Luke was act[ually] wanted to see

But Sarah wasn't sure. They were poles apart in beliefs and value systems. 'I thought you hated the limelight,' she said, avoiding a direct answer.

'This has nothing to do with the limelight. I want a place in your life, not on your show.'

Sarah drew a taut breath. 'My show and my life are pretty much intertwined.'

'They don't have to be.'

She felt renewed stirrings of uncertainty. They saw life very differently. Was the attraction between them, however magnetic, enough of a counterbalance?

'Yes,' she said decisively, out loud.

'Yes?' Luke queried.

Sarah felt a blush starting and fought it. 'Yes, I'd like to see you again. Are you satisfied?'

He took his time responding. 'Not yet, but I've no doubt I will be…'

Valerie Parv, a successful journalist and non-fiction writer, began writing for Mills & Boon in 1982. Born in Shropshire, England, she grew up in Australia and now lives with her cartoonist husband and their cat—the office manager—in Sydney, New South Wales. She is a keen futurist, a *Star Trek* enthusiast, and her interests include travelling, restoring dolls' houses and entertaining friends. Writing romance novels affirms her belief in love and happy endings.

Recent titles by the same author:

A ROYAL ROMANCE

KISSED BY
A STRANGER

BY
VALERIE PARV

MILLS & BOON®

All the characters in this book have no existence outside the imagination of the author, and have no relation whatsoever to anyone bearing the same name or names. They are not even distantly inspired by any individual known or unknown to the author, and all the incidents are pure invention.

First published in Great Britain 1997
Harlequin Mills & Boon Limited,
Eton House, 18-24 Paradise Road, Richmond, Surrey TW9 1SR

© Valerie Parv 1997

ISBN 0 263 80467 4

Set in Times Roman 11 on 12 pt.
02-9711-46613 C1

Printed and bound in Great Britain
by Mackays of Chatham PLC, Chatham

CHAPTER ONE

SARAH barely had time to think about the folly of counting her chickens when her world turned sickeningly on its side.

One minute she was talking on the two-way radio to the camera crew following a few car-lengths behind, and the next she had slammed into a big red four-wheel drive car which had careened out of a side-street into her path.

Metal crunched against metal, the impact throwing her around inside her own car like dice rattling in a shaker. She slammed against the roof, then the dashboard, then the steering wheel, but her seat belt held—although it felt as if it was cutting her in two. Glass rained around her, spattering her skin and hair.

In the timeless silence which followed the crash she became aware of two things: by a miracle she wasn't hurt, although she was pinned by the angle at which her car had come to a stop, and she could smell petrol.

Her teeth ached from the shaking, and from clenching them so tightly. Her vision was blurred but cleared when she shook her head, although the action didn't help the headache she could feel building.

'Of all the stupid, idiotic...' Her mind refused to supply a fitting description for the other driver. The fool hadn't even looked before barrelling out into the traffic. On the Gold Coast Highway, one of Queensland's busiest roads, it was a good way to commit suicide. She only wished he hadn't tried to take her with him.

Through the shattered front window she could see a crowd gathering around the mangled vehicles. Furious enough to spit nails she might be, but she hoped no one was hurt. As a TV journalist, she'd covered enough serious accidents not to wish such mayhem on anyone.

The sight of the crowd sounded another warning. The petrol smell. She had to get out of here and warn everyone to get back before the whole car blew up.

Easier said than done, she soon found. The driver's side door was jammed, and hammering her shoulder against it had no effect. She leaned close to the shattered window. 'Somebody help me open this door.'

Unbelievably, a man was there within seconds, practically wrenching the door off its hinges. As soon as it was open he unsnapped her seat belt. 'Are you hurt? Can you move safely?'

She nodded. 'Mainly bruised, I think. Everything I can flex seems to work.'

She saw him sniff the air then frown. 'Put your arm around my shoulders. I'll lift you clear.'

He had reached the same conclusion she had. The car was no safe place to hang around. With a groan of effort she got her arm around his shoulder, some part of her noting that he was built like a tank. It was a reassuring discovery.

He wasn't even breathing hard by the time he set her down on the grass verge, some distance from the car. She watched in amazement as he left her long enough to persuade the onlookers to move well away from the vehicles. The crowd seemed to recognize his authority instinctively. A military man? No, but definitely a leader of some sort, she concluded, watching him as he strode back to her side. In the distance sirens wailed, coming closer as she listened.

It reminded her that there was still considerable danger. She tried to struggle to her feet, but the man stayed her with a hand on her shoulder. 'Take it easy. You could be in shock.'

'I feel fine.' But when she tried to rise her rubbery legs refused to support her. She sank back onto the grass. 'On the other hand...'

The man hunkered down beside her. 'Now will you do as you're told?'

'The other driver?'

'Being looked after. It doesn't look as if anyone else is involved, which is a miracle considering the stupid way he shot out into the traffic.'

'There was nowhere else for me to go except into him,' she said shakily. To her fury she felt her eyes brim and squeezed them shut. 'I feel like such a fool.'

'Aren't celebrities allowed to have normal, human reactions?'

Surprised, she opened her eyes. 'You know me?'

Humour flickered across his features, which she now saw were more craggy than handsome but incredibly appealing for all that. The eyes regarding her with mild amusement were the deepest blue she'd ever seen. 'You can't watch *Coast to Coast* and not recognise its star, Sarah Fox. My name's Luke.'

'Hi, Luke.' She glanced down at her bruised, tattered state, unwilling to admit how much his recognition warmed her—or how much she wished they could have met under different circumstances. 'Some

star,' she muttered. 'Can't even make it back to the
studio in one piece.'

He brushed long fingers through his thick black
hair, exposing a streak of silver at each temple. The
streaks looked natural but she'd bet they hadn't come
with age. If he was much over thirty-two she'd be
amazed. 'The accident wasn't your fault,' he insisted.

'But the car belongs to the show. They'll…'

Whatever else she might have said was drowned in
a roar like a train going through a tunnel. She gasped
as Luke threw himself across her body, shielding her
as the fuel tank of her car finally burst into flames. A
fireball leapt skywards, the hot wind fanning across
them, and she clutched at Luke, instinctively burying
her face against the thickly padded muscle of his
shoulder.

Screams and shouts erupted over the fire's dragon
voice, and people scattered in panic. The sound
pounded at her ears and she screwed her eyes tight
shut. She felt Luke's hold on her tighten. 'It's okay,
I've got you.'

In the odd timelessness of crisis, she recognised
that he meant it. He wouldn't let any harm come to
her. She felt her laboured breathing ease a little.

Then the wail of sirens split the air as rescue vehicles screamed to a halt around them and workers
raced to attend the blazing car. It could have been
seconds or minutes before they got the flames under
control. Her perception of time was distorted by the
unreality of the situation. But gradually the car was
reduced to a smouldering wreck, emitting ribbons of
yellow smoke which curled lazily into the air.

Luke helped her to sit up. He looked pale but in

better control than she felt. The back of his shirt was flecked with cinders but he shrugged off her concern. 'What matters is that you're all right.'

'Thanks to you—again,' she acknowledged.

His lopsided grin did strange things to her insides. 'Glad to be of service. Were you rushing back to the studio with a hot story?'

He was trying to defuse the horror of what had just happened, she recognised. She shot a shaky glance at the still smoking car. 'Not *that* hot, I hope. We're on our way back from doing a solar energy story at a mud-brick community called Sunville.'

'In the Gold Coast Hinterland. I know it. It borders a property of mine.' He frowned. 'How will you get home from here?'

She grimaced. 'I can't even think about home until I've checked in with the studio. Luckily the camera crew weren't involved, so I can hitch a ride with them.'

Was she imagining things or did he seem relieved that she wouldn't need a lift home? She found the thought oddly disquieting. Already she found herself curiously reluctant to see him walk away.

Whether it was the thought of him leaving her life as abruptly as he'd entered it or the sight of Rick walking towards her wielding his camera, she wasn't sure. But she felt light-headed suddenly. She fought the sensation down. Automatically her hand went to the tangled mess of her hair. 'Don't look now, but here's one of my crew now, and he's got the camera turning. He must have decided we're part of the story.'

Luke's dark gaze flickered to the approaching cam-

eraman. Then he looked around at the crowd pressing
in on them from all sides. In seconds Rick would have
them on film for that evening's edition of *Coast to
Coast*.

'Do you want to have this on film?' Luke asked
her urgently.

She shook her head. Her shoulder-length blonde
curls were a mass of tangles, her skin felt gritty with
cinders from the explosion and her clothes were torn
and dirty. 'Not looking like this.'

'Neither do I. So there's only one solution.'

'What are you—?'

Before she could complete her question, his mouth
fastened over hers. It was just as well he had consulted her, because resistance would have been futile.
It would have been like wrestling with a brick wall
resting on her chest.

'What are you doing?' she asked between breaths.

'Giving you mouth-to-mouth resuscitation,' he said,
the same way.

It was hard to speak when her mouth was being
covered every few seconds by his. It was also un-
nerving to be kissed by a man who already set her
senses on overdrive. Under other circumstances she
could have managed to enjoy having his mouth covering hers. But these weren't ordinary circumstances.

'I know you don't want Rick to film you, but is
this really necessary?' she asked.

'Unless you have a better idea.'

The soft wind of his breath in her mouth and the
warm, compelling feel of his lips moving over her
own made thinking clearly next to impossible. She
allowed her eyes to close but it was a mistake, serving

to focus her awareness even more closely on her rescuer and his effect on her. Her senses reeled. She tried to blame the shock of the accident but knew it wasn't the whole explanation.

When she felt Luke relax, she opened her eyes cautiously, striving to sound more composed than she felt. 'Do you think you put Rick off the idea of filming us?'

'I was a bit too busy to notice, but I think so. A studio isn't likely to use footage of somebody being resuscitated. A bit too graphic for the evening news.'

'Let's hope so,' she said fervently.

'In any case, our faces were well hidden, so you can relax. Your image is intact.'

And his privacy was assured, she thought. Well, the man had pulled her out of the wreckage, probably saving her life. If he didn't want publicity, she wouldn't force it on him. She owed him at least that much.

He sat back on his heels. 'When your cameraman saw me working on you, he went to fetch the paramedics. You should let them check you over. Nothing seems to be broken but your colour's high and your breathing is a bit shallow.'

She was tempted to laugh. The symptoms he described hadn't been present until he'd started 'resuscitating' her. What was going on here? Maybe she was shocky from the accident after all. 'You could be right,' she agreed.

She closed her eyes again, trying to sort out her confused feelings. When she opened them a woman in ambulance uniform was bending over her. Luke was gone.

'The man with me—did you see where he went?' she asked tremulously as a sense of loss swept over her.

Her fingers resting on Sarah's pulse, the paramedic frowned. 'You mean your friend with the camera? He's over with the rest of your people.'

Had she dreamed Luke's presence? It seemed impossible that a complete stranger could have made such an impact on her in a few minutes. What had he done besides take care of her—and kiss her senseless in the guise of first aid?

A tremor shot through her and the paramedic looked concerned. 'Are you cold?'

'I'm fine, honestly,' she repeated, for what seemed like the dozenth time.

She was still repeating it when Rick and the crew yielded to her request to be dropped off at a friend's place on the Gold Coast. 'Are you sure you're all right?'

'The ambulance people checked me over and everything's working perfectly,' she insisted. Everything except possibly her common sense. Why else was she so anxious to track down a man she'd never seen before today? Yet something drove her to try, even if it proved hopeless.

'I'll join you at the studio as soon as I take care of a personal problem,' she promised, waving the crew away.

She stood outside her friend's office, gathering her thoughts. If anyone could help her find out more about her mysterious, camera-shy rescuer, it was Kitty Sale. Kitty ran the most successful photo library on the coast and had supplied Sarah with more useful information than she could remember.

'You realise he could be passing through? He may not even live in Australia,' Kitty pointed out over herbal tea when Sarah had finished relating the afternoon's adventure.

Sarah sighed. 'I know. I have so little to go on. But I must find him and thank him for pulling me out of the car. He probably saved my life.'

Kitty regarded her shrewdly. 'All you want to do is thank him?'

'Well, maybe a bit more than that.' She set the cup of chamomile tea down on a side-table. 'All right, he intrigues me.'

Kitty's eyebrow lifted. 'Personally or professionally?'

Sarah hesitated. She'd been telling herself that her interest in Luke was professional, but in the instant she opened her mouth to tell Kitty so she knew it wasn't the whole story. 'Probably both.'

'At least you're honest. He sounds worth the effort—although your description could fit a dozen dark-haired hunks on the Gold Coast.'

'All called Luke?'

'If it's his real name.'

Sarah pressed her fingers to her temples. Her head ached, thanks to the accident, making it hard to think clearly. Then she remembered something more. 'His hair is unusual,' she said, without opening her eyes. 'He has a streak of silver at each temple.'

When she opened her eyes, Kitty was grinning. 'Silver streaks, huh? Why didn't you say so in the first place?' She dived for her voluminous photo cata-

logues, shuffling through files until she located a
brown envelope. With a flourish, she pulled out a
glossy photo of a man in sleek black and gold racing
leathers. 'Is this him?'

Sarah's heart missed a beat as she took the photo
from Kitty. The midnight eyes seemed to lock with
hers as she studied the craggy face above the leather
outfit. It was Luke.

He cradled a full-face helmet in one arm and stood,
with legs braced wide apart, alongside something that
looked more like a silver bullet than a car. The power
and purpose she'd sensed emanating from him suddenly clicked into place. Her throat dried. 'Yes, it's
him.'

'I knew it. As soon as you mentioned the silver
streaks. They are…were…his trademark. He's Luke
Ansfield and those same streaks earned him the nick-
name "Lightning". He used to be the top Formula
One racing driver—five times world champion, if I
recall correctly.'

Sarah resisted the urge to hold the photo close
against herself, hardly daring to examine her motives.
The man had saved her life. She shouldn't read more
into this than there was. All the same she heard herself
ask Kitty, 'Can I keep this for a while?'

Kitty nodded. 'What are friends for? When you return it, make sure you put his phone number on the
back.'

Something sharp stabbed Sarah, yet she had no
claim on Luke Ansfield. She had no reason to react
so strongly to Kitty's suggestion. She made herself
laugh. 'What happened to Jeff, the one who jumps
out of helicopters?'

'He only did it once, to get an award-winning aerial photo. In any case, I'm involved with Kevin now. He's a cinematographer at the film studios.'

This time Sarah's laugh was genuine. 'Ian, then Jeff and now Kevin. Still working your way through the alphabet?'

Kitty grinned. 'Maybe. And you know what comes after K? L— as in Luke.'

'Remember what you told me. He may not even live on the coast.'

'Neither did Jeff or Kevin. It doesn't have to be a handicap—especially at the speed a man like Luke moves.'

Surprise jolted through Sarah, but Kitty was referring to Luke's racing career, not to what had happened on the highway earlier. Still, the comment had hit so close to home that Sarah shuddered.

'He used to have a pretty wild reputation,' Kitty went on. 'He's supposed to have settled down after he got into some trouble in Europe—enough to make him give up racing, since he came back to Australia four years ago. So it might pay you to be a bit cautious.'

Kitty meant well, Sarah knew. But she sensed that nothing Luke could have done could be so terrible. But it had made him give up a sport he loved. She chewed her lower lip. 'How do you know so much?' she asked Kitty.

'Gavin, who came before Hedley, was a pit-man on the Grand Prix circuit. When we were together I spent some time trackside. How do you think I got that shot of Luke?'

Sarah nodded. 'I'm glad you did.'

'What will you do now? Use your journalistic skills to track your hero down?'

'You never know.' Sarah looked at her watch and started. 'But not right now. I was due in make-up half an hour ago.' Throwing her thanks over her shoulder, she flew out of the building and hailed a taxi to take her to the studio.

Donna Blake, the producer of *Coast to Coast*, was tearing her hair out. 'Didn't the guys tell you about the accident?' Sarah asked, allaying the woman's censure.

Immediately the producer looked concerned. 'You went to a doctor?'

Sarah squirmed uncomfortably. 'Not exactly. But the delay did involve the accident.' It was the truth, Sarah told herself.

The producer looked severe. 'Sarah, the contest for the job of permanent anchor on this show is down to you and Richard Nero. Unless you buckle down and work like mad, you're practically handing him the job.'

Sarah was only too aware of it. 'Sometimes I feel like making him a present of it,' she retorted. But it wasn't entirely true. The anchor job on *Coast to Coast* would be the culmination of years of commitment and hard work on her part.

Starting as a newspaper journalist, she'd progressed to on-air reporter, occasionally filling in as anchor when the show's regular front-person, Angela Fordham, was on holidays.

Angela had been head-hunted by a national network six months before. Since then, the anchor job had been shared between Sarah and Richard Nero. The two of them spent alternate weeks in the job while management and the ratings made the decision.

So far Sarah felt she was ahead on points, but it was no reason to be complacent. Office gossip had it that management favoured a male presenter, although they couldn't admit to any such thing, and Richard's main strength lay in his ability to play corporate politics, which Sarah hated.

Somehow she managed to get through the show, reading the solar energy story from the autocue over the film they'd taken that morning at the Hinterland community.

The final story was almost her undoing. One of the roving reporters threw to a late story and suddenly Sarah's monitor showed the film Rick had taken at the scene of the accident.

It was a shock to see film of herself lying on the ground, intercut with shots of the mangled car, and also to see Luke's powerfully male form bending over her, his lips pressed to hers in the so-called kiss of life. Her heart sank. So much for Luke's belief that the studio wouldn't screen such a traumatic moment. He had reckoned without the news value of his 'patient'.

Her face was white beneath the studio make-up by the time they cut back to her for her closing remarks. For the life of her, she couldn't recall what she said, although it must have been acceptable because nobody commented once the on-air light went out and everyone relaxed.

The producer came up to her. 'You looked pale when we did the accident story. Brought it all back, huh?'

It had, but not for the reason Donna suspected. 'Yes, it did,' she admitted, disturbed to hear how shaky she sounded.

'Just as well Richard's in the chair tomorrow,' the producer commented. 'Go home and get some rest. You look like you need it.'

She went home, but she was much too keyed-up to rest. She had vowed not to look at the videotape of the show she automatically recorded every day. But, as if in a dream, she found herself replaying the accident segment, freezing the tape when the camera lens closed on Luke's broad back. His face wasn't visible, as he'd ensured, but she felt a sudden strange longing to reach out a hand and run it across those corded muscles.

She already knew how it felt to be kissed by him. What would it be like if there was genuine passion in the kiss?

Hold it, she told herself, drawing a deep breath. What did she know about the man—other than his name and occupation, and Kitty's suggestion that there had been some scandal attached to his departure from motor racing?

And the fact that he excited her beyond anything she'd ever experienced before.

Minutes later she was seated at her computer, fingers flying over the keyboard as she chased any remnant of information about the mysterious Luke Ansfield.

He had said he owned property near the solar energy community, so she started by accessing council records of neighbouring landholders. Most of the names were familiar, from various news stories or local events, but one very large property was registered in the name of a holding company whose name she didn't recognise. She would bet her last dollar that company was owned by Luke Ansfield.

Noting the address, she made an effort to suppress her rising excitement and get at least a few hours' sleep. Tomorrow she would go in search of her reticent rescuer.

By morning her certainty had receded a little. What if he did own the land but didn't welcome visitors? She considered telephoning ahead but rejected the idea. If she turned up unannounced, he could hardly tell her not to come.

Having covered the Sunville story, she knew the area in the Gold Coast Hinterland where the property was located. The narrow road wound through the foothills near Nerang to the Beechmont Plateau.

Around her, rolling green slopes were dotted with beef cattle farms. She kept her pace slow and her eyes open for horseback riders. One accident for the week was quite enough.

The turn-off to Luke's land was so overgrown that she almost missed it. She wasn't sure whether she'd expected high wrought-iron gates and electric fences, but it certainly hadn't been the inconspicuous post-and-rail entry that she found. A small sign identified the property as Hilltop.

If you wanted to be discreet this was a good way to go about it, she thought, although the deeply rutted dirt track winding up the face of an almost vertical mountain seemed like overkill.

She had just about given up on reaching any human

habitation when the road opened onto a clearing among the forest trees. In the centre was a colonial-style house of substantial proportions.

Care had been taken to incorporate traditional materials and colours. The building had wide verandahs surrounding its U-shaped design. What looked like a natural rock-pool, but probably wasn't, served as a swimming pool off to one side of the clearing. Picturesque was the first word which sprang to Sarah's mind.

At least here was a residence befitting Luke Ansfield's status, she thought, feeling her spirits lift. She had begun to have serious doubts after traversing that daunting driveway.

Fresh doubts assailed her as she spotted a man polishing a jade-green Branxton cabriolet. Just the sort of car she'd imagined Luke Ansfield driving, but the man working on it wasn't Luke.

The man met her halfway from her car. 'Are you lost?'

Her reflection stared disconcertingly back at her from the car's glossy finish. She looked away. 'Is this your place?'

The man's face hardened slightly as he sensed her evasion. 'I live here, yes.'

Sarah also had an instinct for evasiveness. He hadn't exactly answered her question. She took the plunge. 'I'm looking for Luke Ansfield.'

The man frowned. 'What makes you think he's here?'

'It is his property, isn't it?' she persisted.

The man dropped the chamois leather he was wielding and came closer. 'I think you'd better leave.'

'It's all right, Glen. You could say I was expecting her.'

At the sound of his voice a strange sensation wound along her spine, all the way to the soles of her feet. Luke Ansfield *was* her rescuer. She would recognise that deeply resonant voice anywhere. She spun around. 'Hello, Luke. I came to the right place after all.'

His midnight-blue eyes were masked behind dark glasses and his mouth tightened. 'I had no doubt that you would, Ms Fox.'

'It was Sarah yesterday.' Damn, why was her voice so husky all of a sudden? She'd interviewed royalty without such a betraying effect.

He gave a long-suffering sigh. 'Yesterday I didn't know who you were until I pulled you out of that crumpled car.'

'You mean, if you'd known you'd have let the car blow up and take me with it?'

'Hardly. What do you want, Sarah?'

It was progress of a sort, but his tone was hardly encouraging. She was also aware of the man, Glen, leaning against the Branxton, absorbing every word. Who was he—assistant, bodyguard? Both? 'I wanted to thank you for saving my life,' she offered.

'You thanked me yesterday.'

'Well, I...didn't know who you were then.'

A muscle worked in his jaw. 'Does it make a difference?'

She threw caution to the wind. 'You kissed me yesterday. It's at least worth an introduction.'

He looked as if keeping his temper in check was requiring considerable effort, but he said, 'Come inside.' To the other man, he said, 'No need to loose the dogs yet, Glen.'

Following him inside, she flicked a nervous glance over her shoulder. 'Dogs?'

'Guard dogs,' he supplied, confirming her fears. 'Between Glen and the Dobermanns, I'm well protected up here.'

Well protected from what? Or from whom? Fans from his racing days, or the problem in his past Kitty had alluded to? Either way, Sarah was grateful Luke wasn't making any moves to set Glen or the dogs onto her yet.

As he strode ahead of her into the house she again became aware of his sheer physical presence. Yesterday she'd put his startling impact down to the shock of the accident. But what was today's excuse?

She made herself focus on the imposing kitchen into which he led her. It seemed to be the hub of the house, judging by the vast colonial table which was strewn with papers and a state-of-the-art laptop computer. Dog toys on the floor reminded her uncomfortably of the absent Dobermanns, and the sheer size of a chewed wicker basket made her gulp in dismay.

She brought her gaze back to Luke himself. 'Coffee?' he asked, and when she nodded, he began setting up a plunger coffee-maker. His movements were assured, economical and definitely sexy. A man who elevated coffee-making to an art form, she thought with a start.

In an amazingly short space of time he set before her a cup of the most delicious coffee.

'My own blend,' he told her when she said so.

She looked around the beautifully appointed

kitchen and into the comfortable luxury of the house she could glimpse beyond it. 'This is a lovely home. Do you live here all the time?'

Tension radiated visibly along his broad shoulders. 'Is this an interview?'

The sheer mystery of the man had aroused her reporter's instincts, but she'd resisted the temptation, knowing her interest in him was much more personal. Since she didn't want to admit as much, she said, 'It is news, yes. When the *Coast to Coast* audience finds out who my knight in shining armour turned out to be—'

'They aren't going to.'

His furious denial cut across her so abruptly that she spilled coffee into the saucer. 'I beg your pardon?'

'I said they won't find out because you are not going to tell them.'

She'd known he was camera-shy but this was totally unexpected. 'Surely your neighbours know who you are? Your face isn't exactly unknown.'

'My neighbours mind their own business, as I would prefer you to do,' he stated, in a tone which suggested she would do well to co-operate. 'These days I'm an ordinary man living an ordinary life, and I value my privacy highly. I would have thought that message came across clearly enough yesterday.'

She felt her face flood with colour. 'You made your point very successfully.'

He moved closer and her pulses began to race afresh. 'I could make it again, just so we understand each other.'

She didn't understand anything, least of all him. All she knew was that the closer he came the warmer the room suddenly became. When his arms slid around her, she held her breath. There was no camera, no reason to let him kiss her, yet she knew as surely as she knew her own name that she was going to allow it.

Her heart thudded as he lowered his mouth to hers. When his eyes locked with her startled gaze, the air seemed charged between them. Her thoughts rioted. What was it about Luke Ansfield that practically bewitched her in his presence?

Whatever it was, it was powerful. Though his kiss was light, almost teasing, daring her to pull away, she could no more have done that than she could have flown.

Instead, she felt an urge to rest her head against his chest and let his strong arms enfold her, shutting out the world as he had shut out the blast from her car yesterday.

He stepped away from her before she could do anything so betraying. She released the breath she had been unaware she was holding. 'You drive a hard bargain, Mr Ansfield.'

If he heard the tremor in her voice, he ignored it. 'Then you'll do what I ask?'

'Well, you did save my life,' she said diffidently.

When their eyes met, she was surprised to see something very like appreciation in his sea-dark gaze. 'It was worth saving.'

She looked quickly away. 'Why is it so important to you not to be recognised?'

'Isn't it enough that it is?'

Her silence was a high price to pay for what he had done, but it was equally obvious that it *was* his price.

How could she refuse? To her astonishment, she realised it was also what she *wanted* to do, which was against all her professional instincts and training. What was happening to her?

With a reluctance which didn't bear close scrutiny, she stood up. 'Very well, I'll respect your privacy. I owe you at least that much.'

His gaze remained on her. 'Do I have your word?'

It was her turn to bristle with annoyance. 'I've said I'll keep your secret and I will,' she snapped. 'So there's no need to set your dogs onto me.'

He ignored the taunt. 'I'll show you to your car.'

Her nerves leapt. She told herself it was the prospect of encountering the guard dogs. It couldn't have anything to do with Luke's presence at her side, could it?

CHAPTER TWO

A WEEK later, Sarah joined Kitty for cappuccino at the Oasis on Broadbeach. Aware of the curious glances they were receiving, she tried to ignore them. It was part and parcel of having your face on television every other week.

Kitty leaned closer. 'Have the powers-that-be decided on a permanent anchor for *Coast to Coast* yet?'

Sarah played with the froth on her coffee. 'Richard seems to have the inside running, simply because he happens to be male. If only I could come up with a real attention-grabber of a story.'

Kitty grinned. 'I can think of one.'

'You mean Luke Ansfield?' Sarah shook her head fiercely. 'I gave him my word I wouldn't mention that he was the man who rescued me.'

'What if it comes down to Luke's privacy or your job?'

Sarah shook her hair back. 'I wish you wouldn't ask awkward questions, Kit. Maybe I'm not much of a journalist if my word means more to me than a story, but I only know it does.'

A Ulysses butterfly hovered over the table and Kitty watched it before she said, 'What about Luke himself? What does he mean to you?'

Sarah started so forcefully that the butterfly swooped away. 'He doesn't mean anything to me.

We've only met twice, and one of those times I was in no condition to appreciate the experience.'

Kitty nodded sagely. 'You were so much in shock you made a beeline for my office to find out who he was.'

'All right, he made an impact. But he hasn't called me since I went to his place to thank him.'

Cradling her cup in both hands, Kitty met Sarah's eyes. 'Do you want him to call?'

'Of course not... Well, maybe.' Yes, definitely, sang an inner voice so loudly that it was a wonder Kitty didn't hear it. Sarah *had* hoped that Luke would contact her. She hadn't misread the sparks which had charged the air between them. It was a stronger feeling than anything she'd ever known. His role in rescuing her didn't begin to account for it.

He didn't have her telephone number but he could easily have reached her at the studio. His silence rankled more than she cared to admit, even to her best friend.

Kitty startled her by slamming the cup down hard on the mesh tabletop. 'For goodness' sake, woman. Move into the present. You don't have to wait by the phone any more. What's stopping you from calling *him*?'

Kitty was right, and Sarah had asked men out on occasion. But with Luke it was different. It wasn't that she thought he would object to her calling so much as fear that he didn't want to hear from her at all. As long as she did nothing, there was still a chance he would get in touch.

She was interrupted by a middle-aged couple, tourists judging by their cameras and travel company hand luggage, asking for her autograph.

She gave it with a smile, earning their gratitude. 'Wait till we tell our daughter. She lives up here,' the woman explained.

They left and Sarah released a pent-up breath. 'I still don't understand why Luke hides away in the Hinterland. I know that public attention can be difficult, but there must be more to his decision.'

Kitty shrugged. 'I only know there was something in his past which made him want to escape the limelight. Maybe he just got tired of the adulation.' She grinned. 'You must be the only woman for miles who wouldn't recognise him on sight.'

'Motor racing was never my sport,' Sarah said. 'He looked familiar, but I was too groggy from the accident to wonder why. So many people look familiar to me in my job; it didn't strike me as unusual.'

'But they don't all knock you for a loop,' Kitty said with a smile. 'Admit it, Sarah, he got to you.' She rolled her eyes. 'Not surprisingly. Having the kiss of life performed on you by Luke Ansfield would bowl any woman over.'

'He did not bowl me over,' Sarah insisted with less than total honesty. 'Why are we having this conversation anyway? I'll probably never hear from the man again.'

She should have known better than to tempt fate when a low voice said close beside her, 'Good morning, Sarah.'

Her throat dried and it was all she could do to summon the one word. 'Luke.'

'We were just talking about you,' her friend said, earning a sharp kick under the table.

'Luke Ansfield, this is Kitty Sale. Kitty runs a photo library,' Sarah explained.

He regarded Kitty with interest. 'Haven't we met before?'

Kitty nodded. 'I'm amazed you remember. I used to date Gavin Corcoran who was...'

'One of the pit crew when I raced with Team Branxton,' he supplied. 'Do you still see Gavin?'

'We broke up a couple of years ago. I'm kind of available right now.'

Sarah wanted to kill her friend there and then, until she saw what Kitty was up to. Well, it wasn't going to work. She didn't know Luke well enough to care whom he dated. Nor was she likely to reach that exalted state. He was already making restless moves. 'Nice seeing you again, Sarah—Kitty.'

'Join us for coffee,' Kitty invited. He seemed about to refuse until she added, 'I have to go, but Sarah would be glad of the company.'

Yes, she would definitely have to kill Kitty later. What was the matter with the woman? Matchmaking wasn't usually her style, unless it was on her own account. 'You said you weren't busy this morning,' she hissed.

'Just remembered an urgent job,' Kitty said cheerfully, picking up her satchel. 'See you two later. Have fun.'

Have fun, indeed. A panicky sensation gripped Sarah as Luke slid into Kitty's vacant chair and signalled the waiter to bring more coffee. He ordered his long and black, she noticed, with the odd awareness she seemed to be developing about him. Small things, such as the way his dark chest hair curled invitingly around the open neck of his polo shirt, seemed to leap out at her unbidden.

'You don't have to keep me company if you have other things you'd rather be doing,' she offered around the tightness constricting her throat.

'If I had other things to do, rest assured I'd be doing them,' he stated. 'Right now, this has a lot of appeal.'

'It is a lovely day,' she agreed, choosing to misunderstand. He was only being polite, she assumed.

His eyes rested on her, their sea-depths compelling in the sparkling Broadbeach sunshine. 'Beautiful,' he said, in a deep voice redolent with double meanings. He took a sip of coffee, and the way the steam curled around his sensuously full upper lip hammered through that strange awareness.

'What are you doing in Broadbeach?' she asked, finding her tongue at last.

'I had business in town,' he said dismissively. 'Are you fully recovered from the accident?'

She frowned. Was she ever going to get a direct answer from this man? 'I'm fine, thanks,' she said tautly. 'The studio wasn't thrilled about their car, though, and I'm stuck using cabs until they get around to giving me a new one.' Thinking of the accident reminded her of her amazingly lucky escape. If Luke hadn't pulled her clear...

'You're alive, that's the main thing,' he said, as if reading her thoughts.

'Thanks to you. Of all people, you knew the risk

of the car exploding, but you didn't hesitate.' It was the first time anyone had risked their life for her.

'Anyone would have done the same,' he insisted.

'But they didn't.' She gathered her courage in both hands. 'Why didn't you want your face seen on television? Was it something to do with why you gave up racing?'

'Maybe I've had enough of celebrity,' he said, although she felt certain it wasn't the whole answer. The feeling nagged at her, but he deflected it by asking, 'Doesn't it bother you to have people stare at you wherever you go?'

She glanced down at the table. 'It's part of the job,' she said, disliking the defensive note which had crept into her tone.

He gave her a studied look. 'You enjoy it, don't you?'

She tossed her hair back, meeting his gaze defiantly. 'I worked damned hard to get where I am now. Why shouldn't I enjoy it?'

He drained his cup. 'You're right. There's no reason you shouldn't enjoy it—for now. But when you find you can't go anywhere or do anything without attracting attention, and it becomes impossible to tell if your friends like you for yourself or your celebrity, then tell me how enjoyable you find it. I have to go. Nice seeing you again, Sarah.'

A knife-life sensation stabbed through her. He was about to walk out of her life as swiftly as he'd entered it, and every fibre of her being shrieked a protest. Without thinking, she said, 'Don't go, please. At least not like this.'

'Believe me, Sarah, it's better if I do.'

'Better for whom—you?'

It was said so bitterly that a flame ignited behind his dark eyes. He raked a hand through his hair and the silver streaks glinted in the sunlight before he smoothed them down again. 'I'm thinking of you, Sarah, not myself. You're correct; you do have a right to enjoy your hard-earned fame. My opinion on the subject shouldn't influence you.'

She managed a shaky laugh. 'I think we just had our first fight.'

After a moment's pause, he laughed too. The sound was unexpectedly warm, diffusing some of the tension radiating out of him. 'It probably means we're engaged,' he said.

A strange thrill shot through her, setting thousands of nerve-endings on fire. It took every bit of self-control she possessed to match his jocular tone. 'Let's see, we've kissed—in the line of duty, of course— we've shared coffee, and now we've had a minor disagreement. These days that practically constitutes a relationship.'

He regarded her gravely. 'I can hardly walk out on such a long-standing relationship, can I? Have you had lunch yet?'

She glanced at her watch. It was well past noon. 'I'll have to do something about it soon. I'm due at the studio at two.'

'Your show isn't on air until tonight,' he said.

'But there are promos—promotional commercials—to be recorded, stories to edit and scripts to write,' she pointed out, adding with a sigh, 'You aren't the first person to think that just because the show lasts an hour I work only an hour a day.'

'I've had enough contact with the media not to make that mistake,' he assured her. 'But I thought Richard Nero was tonight's presenter. I gather you take turns.'

It thrilled her much more than it should have to think he kept up to date on her career. It was common enough knowledge, and probably meant nothing, but for some reason the discovery pleased her. 'Tonight's show is part of a charity fund-raising telethon, so we're doing it together for once,' she explained.

'You don't relish the experience?'

She looked away. 'I can't stand the man. He wants the job of permanent anchor and will do anything to get it.'

'And you?'

She felt herself flushing. Surely he didn't think she was as ruthlessly ambitious as Richard Nero? 'I want it,' she admitted frankly. 'But I'd rather win it on merit than play corporate politics to achieve it.'

'You don't think Nero has merit?'

'Of course he does. But ethics should play a part in getting stories.'

'Then it's just as well it was you and not Richard Nero I pulled out of the car,' Luke observed.

She couldn't help smiling. 'Would you have given the kiss of life to Richard so readily?'

His assessing gaze lingered on her face. 'Let's say it wouldn't have been so...pleasurable.' There was a wealth of meaning in the way he said the word. He knew, she thought as warmth pervaded her limbs. He knew exactly his effect on her from the moment his mouth had touched hers.

She felt the blood scorch her face and wished for

a concealing layer of television make-up. As it was, she wore almost none when she wasn't working, so her discomfiture blazed like a beacon for him to see.

'Sarah?' he queried softly.

'I…uh…let's have lunch,' she said, taking refuge behind the café's menu. For a small beachfront establishment, it boasted an amazingly large menu—for which she was grateful as she hid behind it.

From her hiding place she heard the throaty growl of his laughter. The wretched man was mocking her. She lowered the menu, her eyes flashing fury at him. 'What's so funny?'

'You,' he said pointedly. 'The case-hardened TV reporter can still blush. It's quite a contrast.'

'I'm not blushing,' she denied fiercely. 'It's the sun. It's…'

'The sun,' he echoed flatly. 'Not the thought of me holding you, kissing you, breathing into that delectable mouth of yours.'

'Stop it,' she hissed, looking around to be sure no one could hear him. It would be all over the local newspapers next day. Luckily there was no one close enough to eavesdrop. 'If you recall, I did you a favour, helping you conceal your identity from the cameras. I could have screamed the place down, you know.'

He steepled his hands on the table in front of him. 'Why didn't you scream?'

She shook her head. 'I don't know.'

'Yes, you do. You enjoyed it. Both times. And now you're wondering how soon we can do it again—preferably without having to write off a couple of vehicles first.'

She felt her eyes widening. 'You're unbelievable. You don't, by any chance, subscribe to the theory that a life you save becomes yours, do you?'

'It would never occur to me,' he said mildly. 'But you didn't answer my question. Do you want to repeat the experience, Sarah?'

Confusion rocketed through her. Now that he was actually asking if she wanted to see him again, she wasn't sure of the answer herself. He had haunted her thoughts ever since he'd pulled her from the wreckage, but they were poles apart in beliefs and value systems. 'I thought you hated the limelight,' she said, avoiding a direct answer.

'This has nothing to do with limelight. I want a place in your life, not on your show.'

She drew a taut breath. 'My show and my life are pretty much intertwined.'

'They don't have to be.' He took the menu from her hands and set it to one side. 'You're more than your work, Sarah. Once, I believed I was nothing unless I was in the cockpit of a Formula One car, beating the field at San Merino. Four years off the circuit, living an ordinary life, has shown me it isn't true. Your own valuation of yourself is what counts, not world championships or the centre seat on some television show.'

'Tell that to my parents,' she said sourly. 'For the first time in my life they're actually proud of me, because I'm doing this job.'

He gestured dismissively. 'Then more fool them. They should have been proud of you the moment they set eyes on you, just for being you.'

She gave a hollow laugh. 'It's a nice theory. But

when you have sisters like mine you need a lot more
to hold your own in the family. My sister, Leanne, is
a top model, and Isabel, the oldest, is the new political
wunderkind in Canberra.'

He nodded, recognising the names. 'So you have a
super-model and possibly Australia's first woman
prime minister in the family. So what?'

'So the only way I can keep up is to get this job,'
she said, recognising the note of despair in her voice.
'Haven't you ever wanted something so much you
could practically taste it?'

A tightness gripped his features. 'You obviously
know little about the Grand Prix circuit or you
wouldn't need to ask. The world championship is a
heady prize, no matter how many times you win it.
The point is, I went after it for my own reasons, not
to prove my worth to anyone. Your worth as a person
is a given, Sarah, not something you need to earn.'

She sighed. 'Intellectually, I know you're right. The
problem is remembering it when I'm around my family.'

In the last few minutes she had told him more about
herself than she usually told anyone, she thought with
astonishment. It was just as well he spurned the headlines. He could have a field day with her confession
if he chose. Instinctively, she knew he wouldn't, but
it didn't stop her feeling embarrassed as she thought
of how much of herself she had revealed to a man
she barely knew.

Except that she *did* know him, she thought in
amazement. Maybe there was some truth in the idea
that there are no strangers in the world. Kitty believed
that it was no accident who sat next to you in a crowd,

that you had probably been close to them in an earlier life. Sarah wasn't sure she agreed, although she was in no position to argue, but there was no denying that being with Luke felt oddly right—as if they did, indeed, have a long history behind them.

At the same time she realised he had revealed almost nothing significant about himself. 'What do you do now you're not racing?' she asked.

He frowned. 'Do I have to do anything? Of course—your yardstick for acceptability. Very well, I'm a consultant on computerised car design to several international companies.'

His answer felt like a rebuke, as he'd probably intended. She felt renewed stirrings of uncertainty. They saw life very differently. Was the attraction between them, however magnetic, enough of a counterbalance?

'Yes,' she said decisively, out loud.

The sea-dark eyes held hers until she had to fight a sensation like drowning. 'Yes?' he queried.

'You asked me a question. The answer is yes.'

He chose to misunderstand. 'Yes to what?'

Damn him. She felt another blush starting and fought it. 'Yes, I'd like to repeat the experience,' she said through clenched teeth. 'Yes, I want to see you again. Are you satisfied?'

He took his time responding. 'Not yet, but I've no doubt I will be. And so, my dear Sarah, will you. I'll collect you from the studio after you finish work.'

She should have been annoyed at his assumption that she had no other man waiting for her. Instead she felt a disturbing sense of exhilaration at the thought of walking out of the studio to find him waiting.

Under the table she felt his knee nudge hers. It was

a casual, almost accidental touch, but it sent a tremor all the way along her spine. She had a feeling to-night's show was going to seem endless.

CHAPTER THREE

AFTER lunch Luke insisted on driving Sarah to the studio, although she protested that she could take a taxi. 'I've already taken up enough of your day.'

'Will you stop organising my time for me?' he said, a steely undercurrent in his voice. 'If I want to spend an entire day ferrying you around the Gold Coast, it's my choice to make.'

His authoritative tone met the tiniest resistance. She didn't need him taking care of her, but at the same time his willingness to sacrifice his time to her needs brought an unwonted thrill of pleasure. No one had done that before, even men who'd sworn they were madly in love with her. She'd still been expected to fit in with their needs and schedules.

It was almost too good to be true. *Was* it too good to be true? Her hand froze on the car door and she looked at him. 'Tell me one thing, Luke.'

'What is it?'

'Why aren't you married?'

A vision of his assistant, Glen, working on this very car, flashed into her mind. Oh, no, surely Luke wasn't…?

There was an icy pause. 'Not for the reason you're evidently thinking, so you can retract that journalistic antenna right now.'

He slid into the driver's seat and leaned across to

open her door. She almost collapsed into the passenger seat. 'I wasn't implying…'

'Yes, you were,' he snapped. 'Although you have no basis for it. If you must know, I was engaged to be married but a lot of things went tragically wrong. I decided I was better off alone.'

Was this the trouble which had driven him out of competitive racing? 'What happened?' she asked.

He eased the powerful car into the stream of traffic heading north along the highway. Without taking his eyes off the road, he said, 'It's a long story and not very pretty. Besides, I could ask *you* the same question.'

Clearly he wasn't about to say anything more until he was ready. She wondered if that moment would ever come. Biting back her disappointment, she asked, 'What question?'

'Why isn't there a man in *your* life?'

'There was someone until recently,' she admitted, determined to be more forthcoming with him than he was being with her.

'What went wrong?'

'He couldn't handle the publicity that comes with my job. Being called by my surname was the last straw.'

'So now you're wedded to your career?'

His choice of words rankled. 'Just because you walked out on a successful career it doesn't mean we all have to.'

A muscle worked along his jaw and his grip on the steering wheel tightened. 'Thank you for the reminder.'

Desolation assailed her. She was allowing annoyance at being excluded from this part of his life to rule her tongue. It was so unlike her that she blanched and rested a hand on his arm. The muscles rippled under her fingers and she swallowed hard. 'I'm sorry. I shouldn't have said anything.'

His sigh gusted between them. 'No, I'm the one who's overreacting. You're entitled to your opinion.'

But it was a further reminder that he didn't share it, she thought uncomfortably. Would he change his mind about seeing her tonight? How would she feel if so?

'What time shall I pick you up?' he asked, forestalling her concern.

As she named a time her heart did a curious somersault. It turned into a full-blown circus when he leaned across to open her door from the inside. Then he cupped her face and turned her to align her mouth with his, kissing her gently, but with lingering promise. As he drew his lips away he slid a thumb caressingly down the side of her face. 'Until tonight.'

'Tonight,' she echoed, her voice husky. Suddenly what was in his past seemed to matter a lot less than what might be in their future.

It was an effort to keep her back turned and walk into the studio. Watching him drive away would have been too much of a give-away for both of them.

Because of the telethon, the studio was crowded. The usually quiet set where she prepared her segments was flooded with light and activity. The red on-air light flashed over the door, warning her to enter on tiptoe. She waved a silent greeting to the floor crew as she made her way behind the heavy backdrop curtains and up the stairs to her dressing room.

This room was also occupied by telethon performers, who apologised cheerfully as she backed out again.

The only remaining refuge was the make-up room, so she spent the afternoon there, making notes and plans for the evening. Half an hour before airtime, Richard Nero dropped into a chair alongside her.

'It's bedlam around here today,' he complained.

'At least you didn't lose your dressing room.' Why had he been spared? she wondered. Unless management was sending her a message about the anchor position. She searched Richard's face for clues, but he was always so insufferably smug that his expression told her nothing new.

She indicated the evening's running sheet. 'What's this segment marked "to be confirmed"?'

He avoided her eyes. 'It's a late-breaking story I'm working on.'

'What about?'

One of the make-up people shrouded Richard in a cape and he shrugged, indicating his helplessness. Her anger rose. How long would it take for him to answer her? But he closed his eyes and the make-up artist went to work, ending any further conversation.

Two could play this game. She sat back and closed her eyes, willing her taut body to relax as a make-up artist began to apply the heavy television make-up. Whatever Richard had in mind was bound to enhance his image in the eyes of the powers-that-be. She only hoped it wouldn't have the opposite effect on *her* image.

Do you really care? The question seeped into her

mind and she gave a start, earning a reproving mutter from the make-up artist.

'Sorry,' she murmured, and tried again to relax. Luke had planted the question in her mind, she knew. He was the one avoiding the limelight, implying that enjoying her fame was some sort of character flaw.

She didn't agree, did she? If so, she was in the wrong business. Damn him for sowing such doubts in her mind.

Except that damning him wasn't as easy as it should have been. Instead of the expected censure, she felt anticipation at the prospect of seeing him after the show. What then? Maybe she'd invite him home for coffee after dinner. She lived at Mermaid Beach, a few minutes' drive from the studio. It was a glorious evening. They could meander out onto the terrace overlooking the phosphorescent ocean.

How long was it since she'd invited a man to her home? Since she'd started appearing on television regularly it was more a case of keeping them from following her home. Luke was different. 'I want a place in your life, not on your show,' he'd said, sounding as if he meant it.

Her eyes widened. He was the first man—the first *person*—in years to appreciate her for herself, not for what she did.

'Sarah, please!'

The make-up woman's cry of frustration jolted Sarah back to reality. She'd opened her eyes as the eyeshadow was being applied. She schooled herself to behave, and the job was finished moments later. As she climbed out of the chair she flashed an apologetic smile at the make-up artist. 'Things on my mind today.'

Understatement of the week, she thought as she made her way to the studio.

Richard was already on the set—in the right-hand seat she normally occupied. His grin dared her to complain. Somehow Luke was in her mind again, giving her his rare sense of perspective—rare in this business, anyway.

She smiled and took the left-hand chair, enjoying Richard's look of surprise. Maybe he'd hoped to provoke a row on the set to make her look bad. It wasn't going to work.

Well, not today. Today she had a guardian angel looking over her shoulder, counselling her. She had a suspicion his name was Luke Ansfield.

It was just as well. Since they rarely worked on-camera together, Richard made the most of every opportunity to upstage her. He stepped on her lines, read the autocue out of order, forcing her to improvise, and ad-libbed jokes which brought the camera back to him, as designed.

After forty-five minutes of this, Sarah was ready to scream. It took all the professionalism she possessed to keep smiling and treating Richard as her on-screen buddy. Only thinking of her date with Luke kept her on an even keel.

Richard seemed disappointed by the failure of his efforts to provoke her. During a commercial break before the final segment, he said, 'You should enjoy the last story, Sarah. In fact, you should have written it.'

Before she could ask what he meant, the floor manager counted them out of the break. As Richard's opening remarks scrolled up the autocue, a leaden sensation invaded Sarah. Oh, no, he couldn't do this to her.

But he had.

She could do nothing but sit there in agony as Richard publicly identified Luke as Sarah's rescuer. Footage of the car accident was followed by a newsreel clip of Luke on the racing circuit four years before.

Against her will, she sat forward. The first view was from the driver's set of Luke's car as he hurtled around the Suzuka track at the Japanese Grand Prix. Then the camera caught Luke himself, his compelling eyes the only part of his face visible beneath a balaclava and helmet, as he battled Schumacher, Berger and Mansell for lap upon lap.

'Ansfield, the ultimate competitor, manages to pass the competition and take the Japanese Grand Prix,' the commentator gasped.

Sarah released a pent-up breath. Several times Luke had appeared to be inches from death as he hurtled around the tight curves with more than seven hundred horsepower beneath him. Her vision blurred as he was shown climbing from the car to be decked in wreaths.

Dazedly she registered that they were showing a close-up of Luke while Richard read from the autocue. 'Today a mystery surrounds this road warrior, who now lives in seclusion at his home on the Gold Coast Hinterland. Why did he quit when he had the world at his feet? We'll bring you more as this intriguing story unfolds.

'One person who has cause to bless Luke Ansfield's

presence on the Gold Coast is our own Sarah Fox, who might not be with us today if not for this reticent racer. Sarah?'

The camera came back to her. She blinked hard to clear her vision. This was the very thing Luke had sought to avoid. 'You caught me by surprise, Richard,' she said, ignoring the script scrolling beneath the camera. 'Luke doesn't want public recognition for saving my life. Naturally I'm grateful to him, as I've already assured him privately. I'm sure you'll understand if I leave it at that, Richard?'

Her co-host gave a wolfish grin, but beneath his make-up he looked furious. 'News is news,' he said smoothly. 'Although Sarah's shyness on the subject suggests that more than her car caught fire last week. Could the former racing driver catch the Fox? You'll hear it first on *Coast to Coast*. I'm Richard Nero—goodnight.'

Sarah was too incensed to care that he hadn't thrown to her for the customary sign-off. As soon as the floor manager gave the all-clear, she tore her earpiece from her ear and threw it onto the chair, whirling on Richard. 'How could you run that story without consulting me first?'

He shrugged. 'They loved it upstairs.'

'But it was *my* story.'

He stood, dwarfing her by half a head. 'Admit it, Sarah, you had no intention of blowing the whistle on Luke Ansfield.'

She felt her colour heighten. 'Of course not. I gave him my word I wouldn't reveal his identity.'

A gasp came from their producer. 'You did what?'

Sarah hadn't seen Donna Blake come up behind

her. There was nothing for it but to continue. 'Luke saved my life. Keeping quiet was the least I could do to repay him.'

Donna's nostrils flared. 'You're a journalist, Sarah. This is a major story. You should be digging around to find out what he's doing holed up in the hills instead of making deals with him. How long did you plan to sit on this scoop?'

Even Richard looked uncomfortable, as if he hadn't expected so much furore over his story. Sarah gritted her teeth. 'It isn't a scoop. Luke's an ordinary man and he's entitled to his privacy.' She didn't even want to admit to herself why she *hadn't* dug into his background. Was she afraid of finding something unsavoury? No, he had done nothing to warrant such an investigation, she told herself. It would be poor repayment to him for saving her life.

Donna gave a sceptical snort. ''Ordinary'' depends on your point of view. Luckily Richard warned me you'd try and stop this story from going to air.'

Sarah swung on her co-host. 'So you sprang it on me unannounced. Thanks a lot, partner.'

Before Richard could frame a reply, the producer intervened. 'Partner may be a relative term. As soon as management hears about this it will help decide the show's permanent host. You couldn't blame them for wanting an anchor whose first loyalty is to the programme.'

Sarah could hardly argue. From the studio's standpoint, it was true. She *had* put Luke's feelings above her duty as a journalist, which was to report the news, whatever the consequences.

But she couldn't make herself feel badly about it,

disliking the brand of journalism which pried into people's feelings, thrusting microphones into their faces in the midst of grief, pain and terror. Maybe it didn't make her much of a journalist, but she didn't want to change. 'You make it sound as if the decision is already made,' she said with quiet dignity.

Donna glanced at Richard and back to Sarah. 'You'll still have a job,' she said, avoiding an answer.

It was all the answer Sarah needed. 'Doing what?'

Richard spread his hands in a magnanimous gesture. 'Covering feature stories, as before.'

Her heart sank. 'On the *Richard Nero Show*?'

Instantly his face brightened and he puffed out his chest. He liked the sound of it, she could tell. Her heart fluttered as she realised she was left with only one option. She took a deep breath. 'Then I'll save you the trouble of firing me.' Knowing Richard's ethics, or lack of them, she could see it was only a matter of time before they clashed head-on again. And then her job would be forfeit. Why not sooner rather than later?

Donna looked shocked. Evidently she had assumed Sarah would gladly stay and play second fiddle rather than face unemployment. 'There's no need to be hasty,' she said quickly. 'Nothing's official yet.'

'But it will be,' Richard put in. 'Maybe Sarah's decision is for the best.'

He would think so. For herself, she wasn't so sure. Unemployment was a frightening price to pay for defending her principles. But she couldn't work with the man. This wasn't the first time he'd broken a confidence, although it was the most blatant example. Luke had done nothing to deserve having his privacy invaded and his peace destroyed.

If she knew the media, they would be camped on his doorstep in very little time. It hadn't taken her long to discover his hide-away, once she'd known what to look for, and there were far more persistent investigators out there who wouldn't rest until they located Luke.

What would happen then? Would he be forced to find another retreat in order to live his chosen life out of the public eye? Her heart ached. Helping her had hurt him, when it was the last thing she'd wanted to happen.

She squared her shoulders and buried the pain before it reached her eyes. Sometimes it helped to have a news background. Your heart could be breaking and no one would ever guess.

'I'll take my accrued leave until you work out the contract details,' she assured Donna. 'I'll go quietly, so there won't be headlines.' She could almost see the relief coursing through Richard's body as she added, 'The show's yours.'

And much good may it do you, she thought as she made her way out of the studio.

By the time she'd removed her make-up and changed into street clothes, the enormity of her decision began to catch up with her. She had to lean weakly against a wall to catch her breath.

She'd thrown away potentially the greatest opportunity of her career for the cold world of the unemployed. Her savings would tide her over for now, but there weren't many openings for failed current affairs show hosts.

No one would believe she'd resigned over a prin-
ciple rather than work with a man with the morals of
a gutter rat. Richard would let everyone in the industry think she'd lost the race to the better man. 'Man'
being the operative word.

Her mother would sigh plaintively and compare her
unfavourably to Isabel and Leanne. Not in so many
words, of course. But it would be made clear that
Sarah wasn't keeping up with her successful sisters.

Damn. The shock jarring her arm made her realise
she'd punched the wall in frustration. Why couldn't
she have been born into an ordinary family where
making it to adulthood in one piece would have been
considered an achievement? She would have to tell
her parents before they read the news in the papers,
and she knew they were unlikely to understand her
reasoning.

She was evading the real issue. She accepted that.
She could deal with her family, as she'd done many
times in the past. It was harder to deal with knowing
how badly Luke would be affected by Richard's rev-
elations.

What use to tell him it hadn't been her doing? The
results wouldn't change. No matter what Luke
thought of her, it was too late to undo the damage. A
sigh gusted past her lips. Just when she'd met a man
who appreciated her for herself, this had to happen.

For a moment she considered leaving before he arrived to collect her. Somehow she knew he would still
come, however angry he might be. But the coward's
way out was not for her. She would meet him with
her head high, bear the brunt of his displeasure and

pretend not to be heartsick over what they might have become to each other given enough time.

Pretending was the only way to keep her self-esteem intact. Letting him know how much she had wanted their relationship to blossom would leave her open to too much heartache. It was simply not meant to be. The sooner she accepted it the better.

Acceptance was a long way off as she went out to the lobby where Luke was waiting. His face told her he'd seen everything. His square jaw was set in a hard line, his generous mouth compressed into an angry slash. But it was his eyes which drew her gaze. It was like staring at a storm-tossed sea. She braced herself for the waves of his rage to break over her head.

But all he said was, 'Ready? Let's go. The car's outside.'

Cocooned in the front seat of the Branxton, with the hood raised overhead, she turned sideways to face him. The waiting was almost worse than any accusation he could throw at her. 'Go ahead, say it.'

He avoided looking at her. 'Say what?'

'What's on your mind. I probably deserve it. Now everybody knows where you live and what you're doing, and it's all my fault.'

He slid the car out of gear and turned off the engine. The sudden silence seemed deafening. 'You didn't ask to bc in that car crash.'

The concession was so unexpected that she drew a sharp breath. 'Maybe you should have left me in it.'

His fingers tightened around the steering wheel. 'You don't know me very well or you'd know that's a stupid thing to say.'

She'd had about all she could take of accusations,

from whatever quarter. 'Maybe I *am* stupid,' she shot back. 'Maybe I should have used the story myself—then I'd be the one presenting *Coast to Coast* instead of Richard Nero.' Her voice cracked. Saying it aloud made the situation distressingly real.

This time he turned to look at her. 'What do you mean, *you* should have used the story? Didn't you?'

Numbly she shook her head. 'Richard found out through his own resources and sprang it on me without warning.'

His dark eyes swept over her in a swiftly assessing look. 'So this wasn't a clever strategy to clinch your position on the show?'

Despite her inner turmoil, she was tempted to laugh. 'If so, it's a lousy strategy. Not only am I *not* the show's new host, I'm also unemployed. I resigned over this.'

His look stirred a rush of adrenalin through her. For a moment she was back in his arms, his lips pressed against hers in the aptly named kiss of life. Suddenly she knew she hadn't been dazed with the shock of the accident, but by the feeling of recognition Luke had given her. As if their meeting had been more like a homecoming than a fresh encounter. Each kiss since then had only emphasised it.

All this shot through her mind in the split second it took for the anger to drain from his face, to be replaced by such determination that she was shaken. 'Nero isn't getting away with this.'

'You won't do anything rash, will you?' she asked, as a vision of him laying Richard out cold flashed through her mind.

His eyes glittered with resolution. 'Depends how you define "trash". Come on.'

Her pulses leapt as he eased himself out of the car, locked it and took her hand. His grip was warm and firm, not to be argued with.

Not that she had any such plans. Her spirits, so recently at rock-bottom, were at risk of soaring simply because he was holding her hand. Still, she needed to ask. 'What are you going to do?'

Still holding tight, he looked down at her, his eyes gleaming. 'Do you trust me?'

She barely knew him, yet some instinct prompted her to say, 'With my life.'

'Then come with me and don't contradict anything I say. Just play along, okay?'

Puzzled, yet oddly exhilarated by the speed at which he took matters into his own hands, she nodded. 'Okay.'

With Sarah on his arm, no one impeded Luke's progress through the lobby and down the labyrinthine corridors. Only once did he pause to ask her for directions. The rest of the time he seemed to act on some sort of internal homing device, heading for the *Coast to Coast* production offices.

'Have you been here before?' she asked in dazed wonder.

'A few years ago, when I was interviewed on the morning show,' he explained. 'Their offices are right next to yours.'

'Silly of me—of course they are,' she murmured. One visit years ago and he remembered the way like a guided missile? It took regular staff members days to work out the studio's maze-like lay-out.

'I suppose you need a good sense of direction when you're tearing around a racetrack,' she speculated.

He grinned, and something weird happened to her insides. 'You could say so. Normally I walked around a new track to get the feel of it. But I've never had trouble finding my way around. Take me anywhere once and I can usually remember the way.'

All at once her feet began to falter as they approached her office—her former office, she reminded herself. 'Maybe this isn't such a good idea,' she hazarded. She didn't know what Luke had in mind, but it would probably be better if she left quietly and chalked the whole thing up to experience.

He stopped and rested his hands on her shoulders, turning her gently to face him. 'I thought you said you trust me?'

It was difficult to muster any kind of coherent thought when the heat of his hands radiated through her silk shirt. This close, all she could think about was how kissable his mouth was—especially when it wasn't set in an angry line against her. Right now, for example, his lips were parted expectantly as he waited for her reply.

She gave a sigh that was half frustration at her own foolishness and half longing for heaven alone knew what. 'I trust you,' she conceded, knowing it was true.

He nodded in satisfaction. 'Good. Let's do it.'

Do what? she wanted to ask, but he was moving again.

Towing her by the hand, he barrelled down the last stretch of corridor and burst through the door of the *Coast to Coast* office without knocking.

Donna, the producer, sat behind the desk that Sarah

had occupied until recently. Perched on the front of it was Richard, a script in his hands. They would be blocking out the main stories for tomorrow night's show, Sarah knew from experience.

To his credit, Richard quickly turned his astonishment at the sight of Sarah to professional affability when he saw who was with her.

He slid off the desk to more comfortably match Luke's two-metre height—and missed by half a head, Sarah noticed gleefully.

Richard stuck out his hand. 'So this is the hero of the hour. I'm Richard Nero—pleased to meet you.'

Luke's grip made Richard wince. 'Luke Ansfield. Naturally you don't need any introduction, Richard. I'm a regular watcher of *Coast to Coast*.'

Sarah would bet that Richard wasn't the reason, but he drew himself up. 'Thanks, but some of the credit should go to our Sarah.'

So it was 'our' Sarah now, was it? Not so long ago he couldn't wait for her to leave. Luke nodded, drawing Sarah closer with an arm around her shoulders. His grip was like steel—not that she had any desire to break free. Whatever Luke was up to, she was already enjoying it.

'I couldn't agree more,' Luke said warmly. 'I'm well aware of the exceptional contribution she's made to the show. Saving her life was one of the smartest moves I've ever made.'

Richard's eyes narrowed. He was too much the newsman not to sense that Luke was up to something, but it was obvious he couldn't work out what.

That made two of them, Sarah thought. She schooled herself to patience as Richard said, 'Then why didn't you want anyone to know you rescued her?'

Donna spoke up. 'You're being modest, Luke. That's why you kept quiet, isn't it?'

Another victim of those sea-dark eyes, Sarah concluded with an inward sigh of resignation. Donna Blake, normally as tough and outspoken as any man on the crew, had turned to jelly in Luke's presence. If her hair hadn't been so short, the producer would have been tossing it at him. As it was, she was practically batting her eyelashes.

Sarah found the sight mesmerising. Hard-as-nails Donna, going weak at the knees over a man? It was a memorable sight.

Luke dropped his eyes in an absurdly bashful gesture which made Sarah want to hit him. 'I did what anyone would have done.' If he'd added ''tweren't nuthin'' Sarah wouldn't have been surprised. What *was* surprising was the way Donna and Richard swallowed this malarkey. 'It doesn't make me a hero.'

Richard's frown betrayed his suspicion. 'Then you didn't mind the story I put to air this evening?'

Luke's arm tightened around Sarah's shoulders and he shook his head. 'Why would I mind? I'm not thrilled about being tagged a hero when I'm not, or about having my privacy invaded. But it's worth it if it persuaded Sarah to leave the show. Now she has no reason not to accept my offer—have you, darling?'

CHAPTER FOUR

DARLING? Offer? *Darling?*

Sarah had agreed to trust Luke and to follow his lead—but this? The pressure of his fingers reminded her silently of their bargain. She sighed. Being a woman of her word made life difficult sometimes.

Nevertheless, she pinned a smile to her face and snuggled closer into Luke's protective custody. It felt surprisingly natural once she got used to it. And she was getting used to it much faster than seemed wise.

'Offer?' she repeated, trying to gather her scattered thoughts. It would have been easier without Luke's arm around her, but he didn't seem inclined to remove it so it was up to her to control her errant emotions. 'Oh, *that* offer. Yes, I suppose I can accept now— thanks to you, Richard.'

The newsman looked wary. 'I thought you'd be more upset at losing to me.'

'Normally she would be,' Luke cut in smoothly. 'But now she has more exciting projects on the horizon—which I personally think are better suited to her talents. Don't you agree, darling?'

She still wasn't sure what he was talking about, but it was worth a little confusion to enjoy the look of chagrin on Richard's face. He was the kind of man who only enjoyed success when it came at another's expense, she suspected. In this case he had wanted her to be crushed by his triumph. If she didn't care, some of his victory would lose its sweetness. Which was precisely what Luke had in mind, she guessed.

'Maybe we should share our news with Donna and Richard,' she suggested pointedly, hoping he would get the message and share it with her too.

A horrible suspicion hit her. Surely he couldn't mean to pretend they were engaged? Richard would never fall for it. At the same time her heart did a peculiar somersault at the idea. She had never been engaged to anyone, and the notion of *belonging*, on that scale, especially to a man like Luke, brought with it a wave of powerful longing.

She resisted it. Having Luke pretend to love her felt wrong at the deepest level of her awareness. She tensed, hoping it wasn't what he had in mind.

He must have felt the tension radiating through her because he began to massage her shoulder with a comforting, circular motion which sent quivers all the way down her spine.

Almost of its own accord, her head sank into the curve of his shoulder. The massaging movement made her feel like purring. She almost protested when he stopped, but her tension had eased, which was evidently his main aim.

Richard's eyes bulged at the sight of the super-efficient journalist, Sarah Fox, resting her head on a man's shoulder. It was out of character, she had to admit, yet it didn't feel inappropriate. It felt so right that she decided not to lift her head just yet.

'This is strictly off the record for now, but Sarah's going to write my biography,' Luke announced. 'We had planned to give *Coast to Coast* an exclusive preview, but with Sarah leaving the show...' He let the statement trail, but the implication that some other show would now benefit was obvious.

As cover stories went, it was inspired, but Sarah suppressed disappointment. She hadn't wanted him to pretend they were lovers, but, contrarily, she hadn't wanted anything so prosaic as a work offer either. There was no pleasing some people.

Then she realised they didn't *have* to pretend to be lovers. With Luke's arm around her and her head on his shoulder, it would be hard for Richard to draw any other conclusion. No doubt about it—Luke was a shrewd—and fast—operator.

Richard's expression was dubious. 'This is a bit sudden, isn't it?'

Luke showed no discomfiture. 'Not at all. We discussed it yesterday over lunch, but Sarah's so loyal she wouldn't consider saying yes—until you made it easy for her today.'

Donna gave a polite cough to draw their attention. 'About your resignation, Sarah. Emotions run high in this business. Nobody wanted you to resign over one story. We can talk about it, and come to an understanding about your future with the network.'

Richard's indrawn gasp rejected this idea. He had managed to rid himself of his main competitor and he obviously didn't relish the idea of her return, especially with an ace in the hole in the form of a big, exclusive story.

He needn't worry. Sarah knew Donna well enough not to be fooled. She wanted Sarah back *with* her scoop, which was bound to be a ratings winner for the show.

With his leading-man looks and world-beating record, Luke Ansfield would appeal to a wide audience. A book which revealed his closely guarded private life, as well as the truth behind his departure from Formula One racing, was bound to be an instant best-seller.

Only hours before Sarah would have rejoiced in Donna's about-face. Now she saw the trap in it, and spoke up with confident resolution. 'Thanks, Donna, but I'm happy with the way things are. Releasing me from my contract is a blessing in disguise.'

Luke's offer was clearly trumped up to even the score with Richard. But something else would come along, she trusted. Her grandmother's favourite homily came back to her: as one door closes, another opens.

It wouldn't be Luke's door. She didn't believe in miracles. But there would be a door, and one day she'd look back on today as a beginning rather than an ending.

'Exactly.' Luke confirmed her statement to Donna. 'A blessing for me, in fact. Sarah will be too busy working on the book to do anything else, so your loss is my gain, isn't it, Sarah?'

She felt drained, suddenly. Revenge might be sweet but it was also exhausting. She wanted nothing more than to get out of here and end this farce. 'Yes, Luke,' she said meekly. He obliged her with a startled look she knew she'd treasure for a long time.

She couldn't deny it felt good to be escorted out of the room on Luke's arm with her head high, leaving dear Richard with his jaw somewhere around his knees.

Luke waited until they were out of earshot of the

office before he caught and held her, his eyes snapping with amusement. He lifted her chin with one strong hand. 'Now how about a smile? We won, you know.'

In the circle of his arms, it was hard to sustain the doubts assailing her. She mustered a weak smile. 'I suppose we did.'

'You suppose?'

His brows came together in mock anger and she was forced to laugh. 'All right, we did—thanks to you.'

'And your superb acting ability. Nero's mouth is probably still hanging open.'

She suppressed a chuckle. But relief at besting Richard didn't fully account for the elation flooding through her. There was more here. The reassuring feel of Luke's arms around her. The closeness of his face to hers, his mouth a tantalising target only inches away.

People passed them in the corridor and she saw eyebrows lift at the sight of the cool current affairs host in the arms of a gorgeous man, laughing up at him. She knew her eyes were sparkling. She could *feel* the sparkle welling up like a spring from somewhere deep inside.

It sobered her to remind herself that it was all based on a lie. Luke had invented the job to help her save face with Richard. She drew herself back from his arms, conscious that it wasn't what she wanted to do at all. But it was necessary. Now that the scene was over, she wanted to collect her things from her dressing room and leave without seeing anyone.

She especially didn't want to repeat the fiction

about her non-existent new assignment. The more they embroidered it now, the harder the story would be to lay to rest when the truth came out, as inevitably it must.

Luke's eyes darkened as she pulled away, but he released her without demur. 'Where to now?'

She showed him. Her dressing room and the corridors beyond it were shadowed now, the telethon being well under way. She was relieved. How could she explain her actions to anyone else when she couldn't fully explain them to herself?

Still, she felt her heart lightening. No matter what happened, she would always have the memory of Richard's reaction when he learned how his strategy had backfired.

In the haven of her former dressing room, she began to pack her things—mostly make-up, a basic wardrobe of clothes, and a small teddy bear dressed in a red knitted sweater with a large heart on the front. He was her good luck charm. Not that she'd needed him tonight. Luke had been charm enough.

He sat on the edge of a dressing table, one leg swinging free as he watched her move around the room. A faint smile curved his mouth and a devilish gleam lit his eyes.

She slowed her activities to look at him, her smile widening at their shared triumph. 'You did me a tremendous favour tonight.'

He folded his arms across his broad chest. 'I haven't had this much fun in years.'

She picked up the Media Grand Prix Silver Award she'd won for one of her first stories on *Coast to Coast*, then resolutely packed it into the bag, unwilling to ruin the mood with maudlin thoughts of what might have been. 'Did anybody ever tell you that you have a wicked streak, Luke?'

The gleam in his eyes should have warned her, but she was still unprepared when he moved to her side. 'You have no idea how wicked I can be.'

She tried to tell herself they were riding an emotional high after the confrontation with Richard. It was the logical explanation for the feelings approaching flashpoint between them.

When he kissed her she was still telling herself it was in celebration of their audacity. It didn't mean anything. Show business people kissed all the time.

But it didn't begin to account for the flames leaping through her at his touch. His mouth on hers was an invitation, an exploration, inviting her to follow and match his passion with her own. 'Luke, I...' Her voice was strained and low.

'Want me?' His words were barely audible as his lips moved against hers. 'You must know it's very, very mutual.'

It couldn't be—not with so much standing between them. The giddy urge to throw caution to the wind and follow wherever the moment led must be resisted at all costs. But remembering it was well nigh impossible as the onslaught of his kiss crumbled every barrier she managed to erect.

His breath was warm, his body more yielding than she had expected from such stunning muscularity. He made it easy for her to rest against his strength and allow his energy to flow through her, as if she were caught in an invisible force field. She had never felt so vibrantly alive.

'We were hot tonight,' he murmured against her mouth. The soft sigh of his breath slid between her barely parted lips. He tasted of honey.

She closed her eyes, leaning against him, and nodded. 'We were, indeed. You were fabulous.'

His hands moved provocatively against her back, hot and compelling through her sheer shirt. 'You haven't seen the best of me yet.'

His lazily drawled comment shrilled a warning through her. Nor would she—if she had any sense. She might not have the anchor job on *Coast to Coast*, but she had no intentions of following his example and slipping off into the night.

Whatever she did next, it would be something highly visible in public relations or the media. She hadn't worked so hard to slide back into relative obscurity like—*like Luke*. The truth punched itself through her mind.

She opened her eyes and looked at him, stunned at the intensity of feeling she saw there. All it needed was the slightest encouragement from her to ignite the passion simmering beneath that ruggedly masculine exterior.

It would be the biggest mistake of her life.

'I've seen all I need to see,' she said, aware of the desperate flippancy underlying her words. 'You've rescued the maiden in distress and claimed my kiss as your reward.'

He made no move to restrain her as she slid out of the circle of his arms. Breathing only a little more freely, she scooped up the bear mascot and added him to her bag. 'Once I walk out of here, I'm a free woman. Who knows what opportunities await me in the wide world?'

It was bravado of the most obvious sort, but she didn't care. She was grateful for his help in giving Richard his comeuppance, but it must end here. Her reaction in his arms warned her that her body had quite different ideas from her head when it came to their mutual compatibility.

She'd already lost one job today, thanks to her heart. It had been the part insisting that she keep Luke's secret which had enabled Richard to score against her so effectively. Showed what came of thinking with the wrong organ.

Luke braced both palms behind him against the dressing table. 'You mean other opportunities besides the one I offered you?'

She stared at him in confusion. 'You haven't offered me any such thing. I know you told Richard—'

'I told Richard the simple truth,' he intervened. 'I want you to write my biography, starting as soon as you're ready.'

The ground trembled beneath her feet. She hadn't for one moment believed the project was real—wasn't sure she believed it now. Was he playing some game to take advantage of the chemistry she was the first to admit vibrated between them?

'You can't be serious,' she denied, sounding much calmer than she felt. Years of media training again, she thought dispassionately. She went on as if reporting a news item. 'You value your privacy and anonymity so highly. Why would you consider writing a book which would splash your private life all over the place?'

His bedrock strength met her uncertainty head-on. 'Until today, I refused to consider it. But, after your show today, my privacy isn't worth a damn anyway. So why not get on with it? The publishers have been lobbying me hard enough ever since I quit the Formula One circuit. Now I have no reason to go on refusing.'

Because of her. She heard the unspoken truth. But she sensed another truth beyond this one. It was there in the tension radiating beneath his certainty. 'Someone else plans to write your story, don't they?'

His eyebrow canted upwards admiringly. 'What makes you so sure?'

'You. In my job, it helps to be able to read body language, determine what an interview subject isn't saying that needs to be said.'

He frowned. 'I'd better watch my body language around you. I thought it was Glen and the dogs.'

It was her turn to frown. 'I don't understand.'

He stirred restively. 'Since I started negotiating with the publishers I've had threats from two people who are preparing an unauthorised version. They don't want me stealing their thunder.'

'An unauthorised version? You mean they'll make up scandal about you?'

'They can write the truth and twist it so it sounds scandalous. At least if I write my own version I can stop things getting blown out of proportion.'

What things? she wanted to ask. Maybe she would if she had any sense. But then it only mattered if she agreed to become his biographer. And she wasn't *that* crazy, was she? 'So you increased your security. It makes sense. But surely these people wouldn't act on their threats, would they?' The thought of him being in any actual danger brought a lump to her throat.

He shook his head. 'If I thought there was a risk, I wouldn't involve you. But there's a lot of money in celebrity stories these days, so the stakes are pretty high—especially as I plan to donate the proceeds to charity.'

His motor racing earnings and consultancy fees meant he didn't need the book proceeds, she guessed. 'That wouldn't sit well with people who want to make money out of your story.'

He nodded. 'Naturally you'd be well paid for your work. I realise you have a living to make.'

'What makes me different from the others who want to profit from your life story?' she asked.

He angled his head. 'You've shown you won't sell out to the highest bidder. I can trust you to deal with the facts of my life without sensationalising it.'

She inclined her head in acceptance of the compliment but her thoughts were in chaos. Now she knew the assignment really existed she wished she hadn't allowed him to kiss her. It complicated everything.

Her own response, the sensation of drowning in his embrace, meant she'd be playing with fire in getting more deeply involved with him.

He'd also as good as confirmed that there *was* a scandal over his retirement from racing. What if it turned out to be something she didn't want to deal with? A disappointment which would tarnish the attraction between them? It was selfish to want to put her head in the sand, but it was also safer than knowing all about him. That way lay catacombs and dragons, a quicksand of the emotions. Where Luke was concerned, the ground already felt shaky beneath her feet. She wasn't ready to abandon all caution just yet.

'Don't answer me now,' he said, as if sensing the war raging within her. 'I'll take you to dinner and you can unwind before making any life-changing decisions.'

It was the sort of consideration she'd come to expect from him in the short time she'd known him. It told her he'd be demanding but scrupulous as a boss. And it *was* a fabulous opportunity. Surely she could put her personal feelings aside long enough to do what he wanted?

Was it only what *he* wanted? she asked herself as they gathered up her possessions and retraced their steps to the car park. She didn't fool herself for a minute that her desire to accept was all professional. Part of her wanted desperately to work with him on a close, personal basis. Wanted a great deal more if she was honest with herself. For that very reason she would have to think this over very carefully.

Burying herself in his Hinterland hide-away while she worked on the book was not likely to further her career either. Any publicity accompanying the launch of the book would focus on Luke, as the real celebrity.

Not that she'd resent him receiving the attention. It was his life story, after all. But where would she be when it was over? Still unemployed, with months out of the spotlight. Forgotten by anyone likely to hire her even as an on-camera reporter. It would be a case of, 'Didn't you used to be Sarah Fox?'

It would be different for Luke. He could promote the book then return to seclusion until public interest in him waned, as it inevitably would if he didn't fuel it. He wouldn't care if no one remembered him in a year's time. He'd probably prefer it. For her it would amount to professional suicide.

Since they were unlikely to agree on the question, an affair, however fiery, would be bound to end in disaster.

'Not regretting your decision?' he asked as they reached his convertible, which now stood in lonely splendour in the near-deserted car park.

She jerked to a halt. Was he reading her mind? Then she realised he meant her decision about leaving the show. 'I may do once I have time to think about it,' she admitted with some candour. 'But I prefer news-reporting to sitting in a studio linking up other people's stories.'

He unlocked the car and she got in. Stowing her bag in the back, he joined her. 'Then why compete so hard for the anchor position?'

'Partly because it was there and—I'm a very bad loser.'

'Especially to a charmer like Richard Nero.'

She grimaced. 'The rest of the crew will love me for abandoning them to him.'

'They can always do what you've done and leave.'

She regarded him speculatively. 'Was that what you did when you'd had enough of professional racing?'

He kept his eyes on the road. They were heading north to an unfashionable part of the Gold Coast, she noticed. She should have guessed he would prefer an out-of-the-way place to have dinner. It fitted what she knew of him so far.

His next comment was equally in character. 'There

were a lot of reasons why I got out of Formula One racing.'

'Perhaps you should tell me before this discussion goes any further,' she observed on a strained note.

He glanced sideways at her. 'So you can decide whether or not I'm good for your career?'

She shook her head. 'It's hardly fair to expect me to work blind. Besides, the truth will have to come out in the book, sooner or later.'

'Maybe I prefer later,' he said shortly.

'Then maybe you should get someone else for the job,' she snapped back. His lack of trust pained her more deeply than she wanted to admit.

He gave a heavy sigh. 'By later, I don't mean indefinitely. I'm just not good at this soul-baring business.'

She felt sorry for pushing him. Maybe it wasn't lack of trust so much as a wariness about the whole project making him so reticent. They were both tired and edgy. 'Maybe dinner isn't such a good idea,' she ventured. But, contrarily, she knew she didn't want the evening to end either.

'We have to eat. Besides, we're here.'

He stopped in front of a modest Italian restaurant tucked away between a newsagent and a video-hire store. The gingham curtains and slate-paved entryway looked inviting. She read the sign over the door: MAMA'S.

Inside, most tables were occupied by voluble Italian couples. One table had a hand-written 'reserved' sign on it.

As Luke steered her to it a beaded curtain parted and a tiny, beaming woman, with black hair coiled at the nape of her neck, surged forward to envelop Luke in a hug. 'It's been much too long,' she reproved between kisses.

Grinning, he disentangled himself and drew Sarah forward. 'Mama, this is Sarah. Sarah, meet Mama, who owns this madhouse.'

Sarah got the distinct impression she was being vetted. Evidently Mama liked what she saw because she threw her arms around Sarah, too. 'Welcome, welcome. It's too long since Luke bring a pretty girl to his *mama*. Sit, sit, eat, eat!' She took the menu from Sarah's hands. 'You no worry. I know what you like.' Then she was gone, bead curtain rattling in her wake.

Sarah lifted her curious eyebrow. 'Your mother?'

'The mother of a friend from my racing days,' he explained. 'She's Mama to everyone. You scored a hit.'

'How do you know—the hug?'

He shook his head. 'Only a favoured few customers get the off-menu treatment.'

As a selection of the most delectable Italian dishes Sarah had ever tasted began to arrive she started to relax. The other diners showed no interest in her, or Luke. No wonder he enjoyed coming here. She made a vow to remember it when next she entertained friends.

Over a magical dish of linguine laced with succulent seafood, Sarah learned from Luke that Mama's son had been a driver who'd died in a crash. 'He was in a coma for weeks and I spent most days with him. After that, Mama more or less adopted me as a second son. My own folks are sheep farmers in South

Australia, so it's good to have a surrogate family close by.'

Twirling a fork through her pasta, Sarah looked up. 'You didn't think of going back home after you gave up racing?'

His face clouded. 'In the first place, it was never home. I was adopted as a baby and never allowed to forget my good fortune. In the second, they felt I should repay them by going to work on the land when it was the last thing I would have chosen. My father and I haven't spoken much since I started driving professionally.'

'I'm sorry,' she murmured.

'Ancient history now,' he said, although she wondered how deeply he felt about it. Probably more than he was showing.

He offered her more salad but she shook her head. 'It was sensational, but I'd better stop before I explode.'

The corners of his mouth lifted into an appreciative smile. 'You have no cause for concern. You're in perfect shape. And you won't have to worry about keeping trim for the cameras for a while.'

It was an unfortunate reminder of matters Sarah had managed to push to the back of her mind. She kept her face impassive but the hurt in her eyes betrayed her.

'It isn't too late to go back and sort things out,' he said, sensing the change. 'Your producer would jump at the chance to have you back.'

Only because of her friendship with Luke, she acknowledged. As one door closes…she reminded herself. She banished the shadows with a determined smile. 'I wouldn't give her the satisfaction. Besides, I already have a new job.' Stunned, she paused. When had she reached a decision? Then she knew some part of her had never doubted it, in spite of all the logical argument against it.

'You may find I'm a worse partner than Richard Nero,' Luke warned her. 'I'm demanding, a perfectionist, a thorough-going son-of-a-...'

Her laughter drowned out the rest. 'In other words, I should feel right at home.'

His answering smile was electrifying. 'The lady thinks I'm joking.'

She ignored the absurdly fast way her heart had started to beat. If they were to work together she couldn't afford to think of Luke as anything other than a colleague. A gorgeous, utterly distracting colleague, it was true. Never could she recall feeling so attracted to a man so quickly. This date with him might have been an error of judgement—unless she could turn it back to business.

'You wouldn't be where you are without those qualities. I don't expect you to change on my account,' she said. 'Perhaps we should talk about the book—clarify what we expect from the partnership.'

He frowned. 'Tomorrow will be soon enough to work out the details.'

Why did he have to make this difficult? 'But...'

His hand slid over hers. 'No buts, Sarah. All I plan to do tonight is take you home—to sleep, alone,' he added, as if divining her thoughts.

Before she could protest, his cellphone began to purr and he reached for it, casting her an apologetic look. 'It must be important. Only Glen has this number, and only for emergencies.'

He listened for a moment, made murmured comments, then snapped the phone closed. His face was set. 'It seems the media are camped in my driveway. I'll have to make myself scarce tonight if I don't want the third degree.'

It was hard for Sarah to speak around the lump filling her throat. If not for her, he wouldn't be in this predicament. 'You could stay at my place,' she offered.

'Richard's story linked us together. They're probably guarding your building too.'

It was one thing to be on the trail of a story, another to be the target of one. She didn't care for it much. 'Then what can we do?'

He thought for a moment. 'There's an easy solution.' His disturbingly direct gaze settled on her. 'That is, if you don't mind spending the night with me.'

CHAPTER FIVE

AFTER today's events Sarah had thought nothing could surprise her. It took Luke's matter-of-fact proposition to make her jaw drop. The scene at the studio must be finally catching up with her because she felt a tremor ripple through her. She gripped the edge of the table so hard her knuckles whitened.

'What do you...?' She stopped, hearing her own choked whisper. She didn't want him to know how strongly she had responded to his suggestion, even if she was sure he hadn't meant it literally.

She made an effort to sound more composed. 'What do you have in mind?'

He threw her a penetrating glance which told her she'd been read like a road sign. Amusement coloured his expression. 'I thought you said you were willing to trust me.'

Heat flooded through her. How far did he mean to take this? 'For a limited duration,' she reminded him.

'Luckily you didn't specify how limited, because I'll require your trust to get us out of this,' he informed her blithely, his eyes flashing a challenge.

After all, she was responsible for getting them into it. He didn't have to say it. She was well aware of where the blame lay for this fiasco. 'Well?' he prompted.

What else could she do? With forced lightness, she

said, 'I suppose I can trust you for a short time longer.'

Where it would get her, she didn't care to speculate. But they couldn't return to Luke's property, and she would be unwise to go back to her apartment where the paparazzi were almost certainly lying in wait. She had little choice but to put herself in his hands yet again.

It was like being caught up in a whirlwind. Over Mama's protestations, and Sarah's own, Luke paid their bill and then, as soon as they were back in the car, made another call on his cellphone. The result satisfied him, Sarah saw from the upward curve of his mouth and the gratified gleam in his eyes.

Minutes later they were heading south along the Gold Coast Highway. They were soon pulling in beneath the curved portico of Surfers' Paradise's newest hotel, the palatial Mediterranean, which boasted its own white beach and breathtaking views from every one of its nineteen floors.

'This is hardly hiding out,' Sarah commented as a uniformed doorman handed her out of the car.

'It's the scarlet letter concept—hiding in plain sight.' He tossed his car keys to the valet and the Branxton was immediately whisked away to an underground car park.

It was soon apparent that they were expected, because they were shown to a private elevator which carried them to the topmost floor—the Presidential Suite, according to the indicator board.

There were no registration formalities and the suite was opened with great ceremony when they reached it. Luke led her inside, his face showing his enjoyment of her stunned reaction. 'Like it?'

'*Like* it? I'm speechless. But I can't let you pay for this on my account.'

'The owner is a friend,' Luke explained, conveniently sidestepping her objection. 'Presidents are in short supply on the coast this month, so he's happy to let us use it as a bolt-hole.'

'Bolt-hole' was hardly the word. An entrance floor of coral beige marble flowed into gardenia-toned carpets in the living areas. Clean geometric lines, ice-white pillars and ceilings provided a dramatic backdrop for brilliantly coloured art and furnishings.

Angled floor-to-ceiling glass in the lounge and a soaring pyramid skylight set into the entrance foyer allowed moonlight to pour through. The stars seemed close enough to touch.

She moved further into the suite. A heavy square marble table was topped by clear bevelled glass held in place by brass fittings. The brass, with the burgundy upholstery on the dining chairs, highlighted the cream silk of the sofa cushions and lampshades.

A wide, carpeted staircase divided at the upper level of the suite, leading to bedrooms and bathrooms, she discovered when she explored further. A charming gallery sitting room overlooked the living space and the ocean views by day.

She found three marbled bathrooms, each with gold taps and a faucet that provided a cascade of water, itself a decorative feature.

The gallery walk gave access to another two bedrooms decorated variously in opalescent peacock hues, aqua and gold. They were linked by a walk-through dressing room fitted with compartments and shelves. Another of the Hollywood-style bathrooms led off it, complete with spa bath and picture windows, shuttered now against the night. By day, the view would be as astonishing as everything else in this fairytale place.

Luke waited until she walked dazedly down the stairs again, then led her onto a terrace which wrapped around the vast suite. It was dominated by a swimming pool designed to flow around two sides of the apartment, passing under the bay windows of the dining area.

She was tempted to giggle like a schoolgirl, her tough reporter's façade threatening to crumble in the face of what he was asking of her. 'I can't stay here,' she protested, instinctively lowering her voice to reflect her sense of being an intruder.

He deliberately misunderstood. 'You don't like it.'

'I like the *suite*,' she said with deliberate emphasis.

'But you don't like the idea of sharing it with me?' He gestured expansively around. 'There's at least two of everything. We needn't even see each other if it suits you better.'

He would still be *there*, and the awareness would taunt her, she knew. She tried again. 'I don't have any luggage.'

'The bag you brought from the studio is being sent up,' he countered. 'As I recall, it contains most of what you might need, including your teddy bear.'

'My mascot. He's called Fabio,' she returned sharply. Why couldn't he see that the problem was Luke himself? Or was it her? Because she knew what a challenge it would be to share the suite with him, knowing it shouldn't…couldn't…be allowed to go beyond that?

'Then think of me as a larger version of the bear,' he suggested with maddening ease.

In spite of herself she smiled. No teddy bear exuded such a passionate aura. 'What about your luggage?' she asked, aware that the question signalled her capitulation.

'I keep a change of clothes in the car. The hotel's housekeeping department will supply anything else I need. I gather you've decided to stay?'

Her sigh betrayed her. Before she could say more, a discreet knock heralded the arrival of their things. Her bag and Luke's suit carrier looked lost in the centre of the marbled hallway, but the valet gave no sign that it was at all unusual—although he was probably more accustomed to delivering piles of matching Louis Vuitton, she assumed.

The luggage was followed by a waiter pushing a cart laden with champagne in a silver ice bucket, two crystal flutes and a salver of glistening caviar.

'We'll serve ourselves, thank you,' Luke told the waiter, who left, smiling at what Sarah guessed was a generous tip from Luke.

She eyed the repast with suspicion. 'You can't tell me this was arranged by the management?'

Luke had the grace to look abashed. 'The champagne was my idea, to celebrate our new partnership.'

With casual expertise he opened the champagne and poured it into the flutes where it sparkled with a thousand points of reflected light. She lifted her glass. 'To the success of your book.'

'Our book,' he corrected, his eyes meeting hers

over the rim of the glass. 'And to my intrepid co-writer for being willing to venture where no writer has ventured before.'

She drank, but his toast set her mind whirling. Was he referring only to the writing project? Asking would reveal an interest she preferred to keep to herself.

Setting the flute down on the pristine glass table seemed like vandalism, so she returned it to the trolley then looked around. 'I must ring my parents and tell them what's happened before they read about it in the papers.'

'Which is likely to be tomorrow, if the media are already camped on my doorstep,' Luke observed. He gestured towards a telephone on a side-table. 'You can call from here, or there are phones in the bedrooms if you prefer privacy. Or—' his eyes sparkled provocatively '—I can talk to them for you.'

The tension which erupted inside her at the prospect of contacting her parents wound even tighter through her. 'Thanks, but this will be tough enough to explain as it is.'

'Without giving your folks the idea that you've moved in with me as well,' Luke agreed gravely.

The low throb of intimacy in his tone sent shivers of reaction through her. She wished she hadn't drunk the champagne so quickly. It was having an odd effect on her state of mind. 'I haven't—moved in with you,' she stated defensively, wondering what exactly she felt so defensive about.

His casual gesture encompassed the palatial room. 'Look around you. We *are* sharing a hotel suite.'

Her hands began to shake and she clamped them together before he noticed. 'As you pointed out, we won't need to share very much of anything,' she reminded him, needing the reassurance as much for herself as for him. 'How long are we supposed to hide out here anyway? I don't have enough clothes for more than a couple of nights.'

His amused expression said she wasn't fooling him for a minute. 'Two nights should be enough for the paparazzi to tire of staking out our home addresses.'

He moved closer, which was the last thing she wanted him to do—or the first. She was no longer thinking clearly enough to decide. 'Is it really such a hardship, spending a couple of nights here? Or am I still the problem? As your surrogate teddy bear, I promise I'm the soul of propriety.'

It was what he might get proprietorial about that worried her.

'Or is it yourself you don't trust?' he went on with quiet persistence.

'I'm every bit as—proprietorial—as you are.' In dismay she heard the Malapropism pop out of her mouth, practically advertising her thoughts.

He grinned and her heart turned over. 'Mmm. I like the thought of you getting proprietorial over me. When do we start?'

'You know what I meant,' she snapped, her nerves strung wire-tight by his nearness. If he was going to behave like this, staying here would be a very bad idea. She'd known she was vulnerable to his charm, but hadn't realised just how vulnerable until they were forced into this absurdly intimate arrangement. Teddy bear, indeed!

Maybe she would have been better taking her chances with the journalists. The worst they could do was write inaccurate stories about her and Luke. It was ironic that they had forced her into the very situation they would probably have written about, turning fiction into fact.

This had better stop right now. 'I'll call my parents from the bedroom,' she said, seizing the excuse to escape from his disturbing presence.

He gave a nod of agreement. 'Choose whichever room you like. I have no preferences.'

She snatched up her bag and practically raced up the staircase, aware that he was watching her every move. She chose the master suite, not because of its grandeur, but because it was apart from the other bedrooms, accessible by its own skylit passageway.

It was the best she could do to put some distance between herself and Luke, and she was going to need every inch of it if this arrangement had any chance of working.

Since she couldn't possibly ring her parents while she was in such a turbulent frame of mind, she decided to unpack and explore. The room was co-ordinated with a shell motif which recurred in the drapes and furnishings. The shell-shaped bedhead was padded, rich with Mediterranean blues, terracotta and gold, looking towards another wall of windows. Soft velvet chairs echoed the scalloped design of the bedhead.

A balcony led off the room, providing an inviting place to enjoy the night air. West-facing, it would give a spectacular view of the sunset. It was so calm and brilliant outside that she hated the thought of going inside. But she still needed to call her parents—a task she couldn't approach with much enthusiasm.

They had been so pleased about her job on *Coast to Coast*, making it clear she was finally living up to their expectations. She dreaded having to tell them she had thrown it all away.

She caught a glimpse of herself in the mirror doors of the wardrobe and was forced to smile. Anyone would think she was sixteen, not twenty-six and living her own life. Still, it was hard to throw off the need for parental approval, no matter how mature or successful you became. At least, *she* hadn't yet found a way to do it other than on the surface.

With a sigh of resignation, she picked up the phone. Her mother, Gina, answered. Her tone brightened when she realised it was her middle daughter calling. Sarah's father was teaching that evening. As a professor of media studies at Western Queensland University, he often worked in the evening.

'It's very late. I hope nothing's wrong,' Gina fussed. Why did she automatically assume something was wrong when Sarah called? She seldom made the same assumption when it was Leanne or Isabel?

'Actually, something is wrong, Mum. I resigned from the show this evening. I wanted you to hear it from me before you read it in the papers.'

'What are they likely to say about you?'

Sarah drew a deep breath. This was going to be harder than she anticipated. 'I'm being linked with Luke Ansfield,' she said, striving to sound as if the very idea was ludicrous.

'The famous racing driver? What does he have to do with you losing your job? You were all set to become the host of the show.'

'It was never certain, Mum. And the business with

Luke is media hype. You were an editor yourself; you know what it's like.' Her mother had edited what had once been called the 'women's pages'. She had given up her job to support her husband's career and bring up their three children. Now her main preoccupation was with fund-raising for children's charities.

'But it's so hard to get good jobs these days, especially in your field.' Her mother gave a long-suffering sigh. 'What will you do now?'

Leanne, as a model, wasn't even employed full-time, yet it never occurred to Gina to doubt her ability to support herself. 'I already have a new assignment—co-writing a biography,' Sarah supplied. 'I—er—can't discuss the details yet because the project's still under wraps.'

'And *are* you involved with this retired racing driver?' her mother persisted.

'He isn't retired. He's a design consultant these days,' Sarah contradicted, seeing the trap too late to avoid it. She threw caution to the wind. 'As it happens, it's Luke's biography I'm writing.'

Can't you for once be proud of me? she found herself wishing. Tell me you'll support me no matter what I decide to do, without measuring my performance against what you judge to be acceptable?

'Have you gone crazy?' her mother asked. 'You're finally becoming well-known. Why throw it all away?'

Before she could answer, the phone was lifted from her trembling fingers. 'Luke Ansfield, Mrs. Fox,' he said crisply into the receiver. 'I persuaded Sarah to give up the TV spot to work with me. I need her expertise on this project, which is under contract for a six-figure sum. You'll have to hold me responsible if you don't see too much of your daughter for a while.'

He held the receiver between them so Sarah could hear her mother's hasty demurrals. Phrases like 'wonderful opportunity for our Sarah' were bandied about. Luke gave her the thumbs-up sign as he exchanged final pleasantries and returned the phone to Sarah.

'So you see, Mum, it's the right thing for me to do,' Sarah said firmly.

'Wait till I tell your father,' Gina said, her voice rising with excitement. 'I suppose you and Luke are deep in consultation about the new project?'

Sarah shot Luke a wry look. 'We're spending a lot of time together, of course.' More than her mother could possibly imagine. She signed off to a flurry of good wishes, which would probably have been less effusive if Luke himself hadn't intervened. She would have stuck to her guns, but Luke's support had made it much easier. 'Thanks for your help,' she told him.

'I came up to ask if you needed any help. You were doing fine, but I thought the back-up wouldn't hurt.'

She nodded. 'Thanks. Mum doesn't mean to be demanding, but she expects more than the average from us all.'

'Which you give her,' he assured her quietly. 'You have no need to apologise for who you are, Sarah.'

She became uncomfortably aware of the intimacy of the situation. She sat at the head of the bed, the telephone pulled up beside her. He stood alongside, regarding her with almost mesmerising intensity.

Slowly he reached for her hands and drew her to her feet so she was held close against him. Her breathing quickened. She had so little resistance where Luke was concerned. Yet they were worlds apart in their beliefs. Why couldn't her traitorous body accept the fact?

It didn't stop her skin from prickling and heat leaping into her face. A shiver of something she refused to recognise as desire travelled through her, seeming to come from the touch of his fingers curled in hers. In spite of everything, she wanted him more than she had ever wanted any other man.

He broke the spell by turning aside, but the effort it cost him wasn't lost on her. His voice was revealingly husky as he said, 'Goodnight, Sarah. Sleep well.'

As he left, she wondered if she would sleep at all.

Although she tossed and turned for some hours, she must have slept eventually, because sunlight streamed into the room when next she opened her eyes.

Rolling over lazily, she caught sight of the digital clock built into the bedside table and started in shock. Ten o'clock? She never slept that late. What was the matter with her?

Splashes from outside the suite told her the pool was in use. She hesitated only a moment. There was a swimsuit in her bag, legacy of a story on beach-combing, so she got up and dressed, borrowed the hotel's terry-cloth robe as a cover-up, and padded out to join Luke in the pool.

He was steadily swimming laps when she slid into the water, acknowledging her with a quick greeting before returning to his task. It was the first time she'd seen him less than fully dressed and the sight almost made her falter.

He was powering through the water, his flesh gleaming in the morning sunlight as if bronzed. Muscles worked tirelessly, churning foam around him which slicked his dark hair into a shining helmet. His strong hands bladed through the water as his legs beat a matching cadence.

The sheer beauty and power of him took her breath away. She already knew how compelling those arms could feel around her, how commanding his mouth could be when he kissed her. It was daunting to discover such perfection in the rest of his athletic body. The waves he churned up beat an insistent tattoo around her limbs, finding an echo in the frantic pounding of her heart.

If there had been a graceful way to leave the water she would have taken it, but backing out now would be a confession in itself. She willed herself to ignore the turbulent emotions surging through her, and plunged ahead.

How it turned into a race she wasn't sure, but after a couple of warm-up laps she pulled level with Luke. They swam stroke-for-stroke for half the length of the pool, then he moved slowly but inexorably ahead. She had been a champion swimmer at university, although she was out of training now, and the competitive urge flowed back as soon as she realised what he was doing.

He was challenging her!

Exhilaration pumped through her and she put all she had into the effort. He had the advantage of a more muscular physique and a sportsman's training, but she was lithe and lean, cutting through the water with a speed which belied her size. He touched the pool wall only a fraction of a second ahead of her.

Chest heaving, she clung to the pool wall, pushing wet hair out of her eyes. The contest had siphoned off some of the pent-up energy generated by his nearness. She felt drained but happy. 'You're good.'

He gave her a crooked grin which punched through her like an electric shock. 'You're better. I was warmed up, yet you almost beat me. Again?'

She shook her head. 'I can barely climb out of the pool. Another race would probably kill me.'

He grasped her around the waist and lifted her effortlessly onto the poolside, then hoisted himself out beside her. Before she knew what he meant to do, he tilted her back and bent over her, his mouth hovering only inches above hers.

The speed of her breathing couldn't be blamed entirely on the race. 'Luke?' she murmured uncertainly.

'What you need is—the—kiss—of—life,' he said, his voice throbbing with promise as he punctuated each word with a butterfly kiss on her parted lips.

The taste of him almost made her forget all the reasons why she shouldn't get involved with him. His hands were warm on her shoulders, his water-slick body moulded against her. She was drowning, indeed, but the kiss of life wasn't going to save her, not when it was administered by Luke. It was more likely to seal her fate.

Even so it took almost more strength than she possessed to flatten her palms against his shoulders. 'No, Luke.'

He sat up at once, letting his legs kick through the

water. 'I'm getting mixed messages here. Which one should I trust?'

He deserved an honest answer. 'I'm not sure myself.'

A frown stitched across his forehead. 'Why, Sarah? I want you and you want me. What's not to understand?'

She realised she was rolling the fabric of her swimsuit higher along her thigh. It was a mindless gesture but she didn't want him to misinterpret it. She braced her hands behind her, but that only made her figure more defined. With a murmur of annoyance, she drew her legs up and linked her arms around them, choosing her words with care. 'I don't want a casual relationship with you, Luke.'

He brightened. 'A serious one is fine by me.'

Serious for how long? Until she got a job in the public eye again and he objected to being dragged into the limelight? 'It won't work,' she said flatly. 'What we want from life is too different.'

He brought his hands to her shoulders and began a slow, sensuous massaging movement which pushed her self-control to the brink. 'Are you sure we're so different?'

Stop him—shrug off those hands which know how to coax a response from you in spite of your resolve, she told herself. She did nothing, although every sense screamed an awareness of the subtle interplay of his muscles, the susurrus of his breathing, even the scent of his pool-damp skin. She pushed beyond the responses she told herself were purely physical, searching for a way to make him understand.

'You're happy as you are. I'm not. I want…'
Words deserted her.

He stopped massaging her and turned her to look
at him. 'What, Sarah? Success? Fame? A million dol-
lars in the bank?'

She flinched from the coolness of his voice.
'What's wrong with wanting all three?'

'Depends why you want them.' His gaze intensi-
fied, yet she couldn't look away. 'Is it for yourself,
or to prove something to the rest of the world?
Because it won't work. No amount of success will
convince others of your value unless you first value
yourself.'

'Easy for you to say,' she said with deliberate, if
somewhat frantic flippancy. 'You've had it all and
given it away.'

'I still have to contend with labels like "burned-
out" and "has-been",' he countered.

Those labels had been in her mother's voice until
Luke himself had spoken to her. 'It doesn't bother
you?'

'Bothers the hell out of me, but I can't change what
people choose to think. All I can do is live my life,
my way. Are your sisters happy, Sarah?'

It was an odd question, and Sarah had to think before she answered it. Leanne had been married once
but it hadn't worked out. Now she lived with the photographer who had helped catapult her to modelling
fame.

Isabel was wedded to her political career, and as
far as Sarah knew had never had a serious relationship. She was too afraid of making a wrong choice
which would blight her future chances of high office.

Luke watched the interplay of emotions across her face. 'Both your sisters are wealthy and successful. Your parents are proud of them. By your reasoning, they have it all.'

She stood up, water streaming down her legs to pool at her feet like tears. 'This is precisely why I won't get involved with you, Luke. We'd always be arguing over these issues.'

'And settling them in bed,' he added, a wicked gleam lighting his eyes. 'Is it such a terrible prospect?'

It wasn't terrible at all, and her heated expression told him so. But a successful relationship needed more than sublime sex. Kissing and making up would no doubt be as wonderful as his teasing expression promised, but what if they never got to the making up part?

She pulled the robe around her body, aware that she was shaking—but not because she was still damp from her swim. He had brought up issues she had buried since she'd started to climb the ladder in television. Yes, she wanted a secure relationship, and, yes, she wanted children of her own.

But she didn't want them to be substitutes for the glittering prizes of success. Luke thought of them as prizes in themselves. He could afford to think so because he had already achieved everything he wanted in life. He had been world champion at his sport not once, but five times. His face was known in every country of the world where the pinnacle of motor racing was revered. Yet he had given it all up to live an ordinary life.

She couldn't afford to let him seduce her with his

words, far less with his tantalising mouth, giving hands and magnificent body. Even so, it was all she could do to walk into the suite and not look back.

CHAPTER SIX

LUKE made no further reference to their conversation, but seemed to be making an effort to keep the mood light. Trying to show her how wonderful things could be between them? Sarah already suspected it, but it didn't change reality.

The newspapers arrived with the brunch Luke had ordered. 'Is it as bad as we thought?' she asked, between mouthfuls of fresh croissant and fragrant herbed omelette.

He passed a paper across to her. 'See for yourself.'

The story was only a fraction smaller than the one on the latest mid-east crisis. Under the headline SPEED ACE'S SECRET LIFE was a photo of Luke in racing leathers, taken before his retirement, and a shot of Hilltop—taken with a long lens through the trees, no doubt.

A sidebar carried a studio portrait of Sarah and told how 'publicity-shy Formula One champ, Luke Ansfield' had saved her life.

Details of his reclusive life in the Gold Coast Hinterland and interviews with neighbours completed the barrage. She tossed the paper aside in disgust. 'Is yours any better?'

He shook his head. 'The language is marginally less sensational but it's all here, including the fact that we couldn't be contacted for comment last night.'

'Thank goodness,' she said heartily.

'It didn't stop them making up the details of our supposed affair.'

Or suggesting she had left *Coast to Coast* because she'd been 'swept off her feet by the race ace', she noticed with a wry grimace.

There was even a quote from Richard Nero, implying that he would have exclusive details of the romance on *his* programme. In his dreams.

She was startled when Luke swept the newspapers up into an untidy armful and carried them inside. How he must hate the fanfare, she thought. And all because he had come to her rescue. It didn't seem fair.

When he strode back onto the terrace, she braced herself to deal with his anger. Instead, he poured more of the delicious freshly brewed coffee for them both and said, 'Let's talk about the book.'

She stirred cream into her coffee and decided to take the bull by the horns. 'This won't go away, Luke. When word gets out that you're doing a biography, the hype will start all over again.'

His face remained impassive. 'I can always leave town and come back when the fuss dies down.'

'Then why write a book at all, if you loathe the attention?'

He swung his chair back until it was balanced precariously on two legs. 'Like I said, I can't stop the unauthorised biography being written. But I can write my own version and make sure it's the accurate one.'

Almost against her will, she read the tense set of his body. 'Including the real reason why you hate publicity so much?' she hazarded.

He strode to the parapet and clamped his hands around it, staring out to sea for long moments before he replied. 'Reading my body language again, Sarah? What is it telling you right now?'

'You've got "no trespassing" written all over you,' she said reluctantly. 'I just can't figure out whether it's the idea of the book itself or what you're going to have to reveal in it that's bothering you.'

He gave a hollow laugh. 'Very perceptive, Ms Fox. Which do you think it is?'

'Without knowing more of your history, I don't know. Were you in gaol? Caught cheating on the race-track? Up to your ears in gambling debts? Hooked on drugs or alcohol?'

A shadow darkened his craggy features. 'They aren't the worst secrets a man can have.'

'Have you killed someone?'

It was said half in jest, and she was unprepared for the ice in his tone as he said, 'Would it change things between us if I had?'

Iced water trickled down her spine. Granted, she didn't know him very well, but what she did know made the idea inconceivable. Was he saying it to test her commitment to the project? If so, it was a test she could do without.

It was said that anyone could kill, given sufficient provocation, but she couldn't conceive of any provocation which would turn Luke Ansfield into a murderer. There had to be another explanation, and she would find it out in the course of writing the book.

Another thought gripped her. Whatever his secret, it was obvious he needed someone to share it with, someone safe. 'You asked me to trust you. So far I have no reason to change my decision,' she said, her voice shaking only slightly.

Some of his tension ebbed away visibly and he took her hands. 'Thank you, Sarah.'

As the heat in his grip radiated through her Sarah wondered if she would live to regret her vow. Not because of anything in his past, but because she seemed to have taken another step closer to him, a step she wasn't at all sure was a good idea.

She forced her mind back to business matters. 'What days and hours will we spend writing together?'

He took a seat opposite her. 'Twenty-four hours a day some days. Other days none at all. You can sleep till noon.'

Suspicion began to wash over her. 'Sleep till noon where?'

'At Hilltop, of course. I don't have another office. I thought you understood.'

A shock wave travelled through her. She was starting to understand all too well. 'I have no problems working at your home, but...'

'Living there bothers you?'

It was her turn to jump up, almost upsetting the table. 'It doesn't bother me because I don't intend to move in with you.'

'Why not?'

She didn't care if her body language betrayed her. He already knew she was attracted to him, as well as all the reasons why she couldn't give in to it. Moving in with him for whatever reason would make resistance all but impossible.

Unless that was what he had in mind.

'I've already told you I don't want to get involved with you,' she stated.

He seemed unperturbed. 'So you keep telling me. At least your voice does. Every time I touch you I get a different answer.'

Damn her body for giving her away. 'All the more reason to keep this strictly professional.'

'A bodyguard and a pair of Dobermanns should ease your mind.'

Against her will, she smiled. 'They're on your side.'

'They'll guard you with their lives if I tell them to.'

She was still sceptical. 'Even against you?'

He made a heart-crossing gesture. 'Even against me.'

She was mad to think of agreeing, yet the longer Luke talked the more logical he made the move seem. In order to make use of the notes he'd already made she would need access to his computer system, as well as to the confidential files he kept at Hilltop.

Try as she might to silence the voice, she could almost hear her parents saying, You gave up *Coast to Coast* to move in with some has-been racing driver? *Sure* you're writing his memoirs.

It was to silence those voices, and her own inner doubts, as much as to make the project work that she agreed. She was an adult, quite capable of controlling her own hormones. If she didn't want anything to happen between her and Luke then nothing would.

She glanced across at him. Bent over the laptop computer he'd had sent up from his car, he looked heart-wrenchingly handsome. A lock of dark hair fell across his brow, which was furrowed with concentration. Still, he looked as if he'd be more at home grasping a steering wheel than operating a keyboard with two fingers which stabbed at the keys with accusatory gestures.

'You only want my help with the book so you won't have to do the typing,' she thought aloud.

His answering grin twisted something inside her. 'I want your help so I won't have to *write* the blessed book. I'd far rather tear around the track at Monza at two hundred Ks an hour than try and string more than two paragraphs together for publication.'

The thought that he might actually *need* her was novel and disturbing. It was bad enough trying to deal with the chemistry which flowed between them like an electrical field without having him throw more spanners into the works. Like admitting he needed her.

It was almost impossible not to respond to the teasing warmth in his expression. Automatically Sarah's pulses picked up speed. She wished she had something useful to do, but her bag of tricks from the studio hadn't included so much as a paperback book.

With Luke close by, she wouldn't have been able to concentrate on a book anyway.

She uncoiled from the chaise longue and stretched, trying to look lazily unconcerned. 'I'm going to get some exercise before I do something silly—like volunteer to type whatever you're working on.'

'It's a list of specs for a new car design,' he said, then frowned. 'Should you go out? The point of staying here is to keep a low profile till the fuss dies down.'

'If my profile gets any lower, I'll be a puddle on the floor,' she vowed. She could hardly admit that he was the reason she needed to get out of here.

She went to her bedroom and returned wearing a flower-trimmed straw sunhat and dark glasses. The hat had last been used on *Coast to Coast* in a story on sun protection. It was hardly her style but made a useful disguise.

Her Pearl Jam T-shirt and white linen trousers were unlikely to attract undue attention.

She spun around in front of Luke. 'What do you think?'

Idiot! The whole point was to put some much needed space between them, and here she was inviting what turned into a leisurely appraisal of her.

'Beautiful,' he murmured when it was over.

'You didn't even look at the hat and glasses,' she accused him.

His eyebrow canted upwards in a 'who, me?' look which made no attempt to conceal the appreciation in his gaze. 'Didn't I? Too many other distractions. But, since you ask, the hat isn't really your style.'

'Thank you,' she said, as if he'd paid her a compliment. At some level she knew she'd have been disappointed if he'd said the dowdy hat looked terrific. When was she going to be satisfied with a response from him?

'I'll only go as far as the shops in the lobby,' she promised, and let herself out before he could talk her into sticking around.

No one gave her a second glance as she browsed in the upmarket shopping arcade on the hotel's ground floor. Accustomed to turning heads wherever she went, she found the experience disquieting. Which proved how right she was not to get involved with

Luke. His passion for keeping a 'low profile', as he called it, wouldn't suit her for very long.

At the same time she refused to think Luke might be right when he said she courted the recognition. Enjoying it as a mark of achievement was quite a different thing.

Annoyed to find him infiltrating her thoughts even here, she turned into the closest shop to hand; a boutique of exquisite fashions by local designers.

Suddenly she felt what her sister, Leanne, called the urge to splurge. It was crazy, given that she no longer had a job. But while she was employed she'd been prudent, and she now owned her apartment, with a little in the bank for a rainy day. Why not indulge herself?

To the delight of the boutique owner, she tried on several garments and finally chose a blouse figured in coral and gold with a side tie, and a pair of fabulous matching palazzo pants.

Another impulse made her instruct the owner to package her own clothes and remove the tags from the new outfit. It was far more eye-catching than the T-shirt and trousers, but she was only taking the elevator back to the suite.

She wanted to keep the clothes on for her own sake, she told herself determinedly. Her body sang a different song but she ignored it, along with the sizzling feeling racing along her veins as she thought of Luke's reaction when he saw her.

She had to skirt a crowd of tourists to reach the elevators, and then wait while the throng cleared before she could unlock the private lift to her floor. Blinded by flashbulbs as the tourists photographed one another, she was thankful when the lift doors closed on blessed silence.

Then it dawned on her that the flashbulbs wouldn't have bothered her if she'd been wearing the hat and dark glasses. She knew exactly where they were—on a chair in the changing room of the boutique.

She needn't have worried about Luke's reaction. He was nowhere in sight. Returning her old clothes to the bedroom, she heard the shower running in his bathroom along the hallway, and the sound of him singing what sounded like light opera.

Some printouts from Luke's computer lay on a table in the living room. She leafed through them curiously. The sleek new vehicle he was designing looked more like a missile than a car. The engine specifications alongside the designs might have been written in a foreign language for all they meant to her, but the authority in the work was obvious. The designs for the bodywork of the car were practically works of art.

No, more like labours of love, she thought. Never mind things like aerodynamic innovation—Luke's heart was in this design. No wonder he had no need to profit from a book. Despite her limited experience, she could see that his skills were breathtaking.

'If it is as good and travels as dynamically in the endurance runs as it looks on paper, it should be a top performer,' Luke said, interrupting her study of his notes.

Looking up, she felt a tightness grip her lungs, as if someone was hugging her fiercely. Fresh from the shower, he had a towel wrapped around his midsection and was drying his hair with another. Her presence bothered him not at all, although his bothered her a great deal.

'Something wrong?' he queried when she remained silent.

Her throat dried but she refused to swallow. 'Nothing. I—er—hope you don't mind me reading these?'

He seemed not to notice her discomfiture as he finished towelling his hair and draped the towel over one shoulder. 'I don't mind, provided you keep the details to yourself. Team Branxton won't unveil this model until the shake-down tests at Estoril. Car design, like race and pit-stop strategy, are kept secret to avoid piracy.'

She nodded, but her mind wasn't on car design. Rather on senseless details like the trail of damp prints he'd left and the way his wet hair gleamed in the afternoon sunlight. She should have stayed away longer—like the rest of her life.

He padded to the bar and helped himself to a club soda, pouring one for her when she nodded acceptance. When he handed her the drink their fingers brushed, and an electric awareness arced through her. The liquid sloshed in the glass with the force of her trembling.

'You look different,' he said in a low voice. 'New outfit. Classy, like its owner.'

All but paralysed, she forced her head up. 'I like it.'

He regarded her from under lowered lids. 'News for you—you're not the only one.'

It was the reaction she had sought, deny it though she might. Yet his compliment provoked a surge of anger, mostly with herself for caring so much about his opinion.

Indecision tore through her. She was caught between wanting him to make love to her and wanting to put as much distance between them as she could. The paradox was killing and she sagged against him.

He caught her and held her up. 'I'd better get dressed.'

'Yes.' It was the last thing she wanted to say.

When he'd gone upstairs, she threw herself onto a chair, her thoughts whirling. She would have to tell him the deal was off. He could find another writer, one who wouldn't care about working under his roof. She could recommend several male writers.

That his choice might be *female* made her think again. She didn't want to work with him, yet she didn't want another woman writing his book. What in the name of sweet reason *did* she want?

Before she could puzzle it out the telephone purred at her elbow. Since no one knew she was here, she waited for Luke to pick it up in the bedroom. A few moments later he came downstairs looking grim.

'That was a reporter from the *Gold Coast Herald*, wanting a story to go with a photo of you taken in this hotel.'

'But I didn't...' She blanched, then worked it out. 'The flashbulbs going off in the lobby. The reporter must have been among the tourists waiting for the lift.'

He nodded. 'He said he was attending a seminar in this hotel when he snapped you. The quote I gave him won't be very printable.'

He was a picture of pent-up annoyance, looking as

if the suite, large as it was, was barely big enough to
contain the energy firing through him. 'Makes it pretty
pointless staying here now.'

Her own anger welled brightly. 'This is ridiculous.
You'd think we were film stars, the attention we're
generating.'

His lips thinned. 'Close enough.'

He didn't seem to blame her and yet she couldn't
help feeling responsible. If she hadn't gone shopping
and left her hat and dark glasses in the boutique...
She cut off the futile if-onlys. 'Is this what it was like
for you before?'

He combed his hair with his fingers, emphasising
the trademark silver streaks. 'Some of it was my own
fault. I played as hard as I drove in those days. I've
mellowed now, of course.'

If this was mellow, he must have been dynamite
then! An involuntary shiver claimed her. 'All the
same...'

'All the same, I didn't deserve to be hounded. After
I equalled Fangio's old record, I couldn't go out in
public without someone aiming a camera at me.
Sometimes I didn't have to go out. A Spanish newspaper once ran pictures of me taking a shower.'

She caught her breath, her imagination running riot.
'Nude?'

He flickered an eyebrow. 'It is the way I usually
shower.' Then he relented, smiling fractionally. 'I
thought I'd put this kind of circus behind me.'

'Until I landed you in the deep end.'

'Landed both of us,' he amended. He set his shoulders in a 'to hell with it' gesture. 'At least this time
I'm in pleasant company.'

Liking the way he made them a team, she picked up on his mood. 'And we can be thankful I wasn't in the shower.'

He sobered abruptly. 'It wouldn't have paid them.'

Some instinct told her there was more going on here than today's incident. Was it linked to the secret buried in Luke's past? Now didn't seem the time to ask.

'It will pass,' she assured him, knowing her own kind. 'Tomorrow some other so-called celebrity will be front-page news. Why give them the satisfaction of letting them know they bother us?'

'Something I have no intention of doing,' he observed. 'But since our cover is well and truly blown we may as well get out of here.'

Sarah agreed with an alacrity which didn't surprise her. She had been wondering how she was to survive another night sharing the suite with him. At least back at his property she would have his bodyguard and the two Dobermanns coming between them.

She only hoped it would be enough.

CHAPTER SEVEN

THREE weeks of working alongside Luke at Hilltop hadn't eased Sarah's concerns. If anything she was becoming even more entwined with him, and finding she enjoyed it far more than was good for her.

They had slipped into an easy routine of rising early for a swim, which inevitably ended up as a race, followed by a substantial breakfast cooked and served by Glen, who turned out to be much more than a bodyguard. He was also chef, manager of the property, dog-handler and Luke's right-hand man.

She and Luke would work on the book for the next six hours or so, eating a sandwich lunch on a tray while they worked.

Actually, 'worked' wasn't the term she would use, so much as 'sparred'. Luke had an encyclopaedic memory for events from years before and could colour them with anecdotal material which set her journalist's mind afire with ideas.

Unfortunately, he was in favour of writing the book chronologically, sticking to the unvarnished facts. Her reporter's instinct urged her to arrange events for interest's sake, not necessarily starting at the beginning, but at the point which she felt would capture a reader's attention.

Sometimes they disagreed so vehemently on the form and content of the project that it was a wonder progress was made. But made it was.

'Do you want this book to sell or not?' she asked him point-blank after one such altercation.

'To quote a noted literary figure: frankly, Sarah, I don't give a damn.'

Shocked, she stared at him. Had she heard right? 'Then why are we slaving over the manuscript?' He must know by now that it was in her nature to put a hundred and ten per cent into any project, to make it better than good if possible. If he wanted her to do less, he'd picked the wrong writing partner.

'The book needs to be written, but I want it to sell on merit, not on sensationalism.'

She lifted the hair off the back of her neck and let it drop. 'We've covered your early life and how you got into motor racing. But that's only half the story. There's still the other half, the part you don't really want to discuss—even with me.' She drew a deep breath. 'The other writers won't be so squeamish about telling the whole story.'

He looked thunderous. 'The one they think they know.'

Her eyes widened with appeal. 'Then tell your side. Before we started this book you asked me to trust you. Isn't it time you trusted me? Starting with the information the other writers might have dredged up about you.'

He gave a sigh of frustration and flicked off his computer. 'We're both tired and irritable. I'm for taking the dogs and getting out of here.'

The message was clear. She could come with him or not as she chose, but the discussion was ended. She fought down a bitter sense of disappointment. She hadn't realised how much she wanted Luke's trust until he withheld it.

He had withheld almost nothing else from her since she came to Hilltop. They had expected to have to run a media gauntlet, but Glen had solved that problem by planting a rumour that Luke and Sarah were holidaying on a certain Barrier Reef island.

By the time the reporters discovered the truth, the story had lost its novelty value. As Sarah had predicted, a forthcoming state election had replaced them in the headlines.

In spite of her reservations, she had settled in quickly. Being able to return home and collect her laptop computer and a more adequate wardrobe had helped. Living at Hilltop was like being on holiday, the work notwithstanding.

She loved the long walks they took every day to work out the kinks of hunching over their computers. Each day Luke showed her a different aspect of his kingdom, from groves of palm-like Cycads, which he told her survived from the age of the dinosaurs, to stands of towering Antarctic Beech thousands of years old.

As well, there was the enchanting wildlife; the doe-faced wallabies, lorikeets, kookaburras, cockatoos, and scurrying families of scrub turkeys.

Luke had even shared with her his favourite feature of Hilltop, a massive fig tree hidden in the depths of the forest. It had a root system stretching tens of metres along the grounds. Entwined with creepers and patchily covered with velvety green moss, the trunk contained a cavity as large as a room.

In this secret bower, to the musical notes of the

whipbirds high among the branches and the occasional call of a shy fairy-wren, he had taken her into his arms.

He hadn't kissed her since that teasing moment by the pool at the hotel. This had been different somehow. The cavern had woven a unique magic around her. She'd felt like a wood nymph, a spirit. Melting into Luke's arms had happened in a moment out of time. Maybe she had even dreamed it.

It was worthy of a dream, the way his lips had roved over her eyelids and down her nose, finding her mouth with gentle, questing movements. Her breath had caught in her throat. She'd found her arms travelling up to link behind his neck and draw his head down so she could return the warm pressure, measure for measure.

There had been no fireworks. This time the heat had banked slowly but inexorably inside her, until it had become an inferno of hopes, desires and dreams.

She'd closed her eyes and the flames had leapt higher. This was what she had feared most from being with Luke, this neediness which threatened to consume her. No man had wrung such a feeling from her before. She didn't want it now. Luke was a wonderful companion. Why couldn't they remain friends and colleagues? Then there would be no problem because her choice of lifestyle was at odds with his.

Turning off emotion wasn't as easy as turning off a tap. He didn't even have to touch her. A glance was enough to trigger a deep sense of longing. Having him kiss her had been like being lost in the desert and discovering that a water-hole wasn't a mirage.

Turmoil ripped through her as she relived the kiss.

Never before had her mind and heart been at such odds. Sometimes she thought she should simply give in to her feelings and have a wildly passionate affair with him. Then move on. It happened nowadays. Love didn't have to be 'till death did you part.

But what if you wanted it to be? She was terrified that once she gave herself to Luke, his memory would forever stand between her and her ambitions. Even if she moved on, she would be less than heart-whole. And she couldn't achieve all that she wanted to if part of her kept looking back.

'I'll skip the walk today,' she said, coming back to the present with a jolt. 'This chapter needs some heavy editing.'

His eyes glinted with the look of knowing her too well. 'It will keep.'

She glanced away. 'I'd rather work on it while the shape is fresh in my mind.' Before other demands drove it right out of her thoughts.

His look became shuttered. 'Very well, but don't work too hard. Fangio, Jackie—walk.'

At their master's tone, the Dobermanns leapt up and beat him to the door. Named after famous racing drivers, they were speed-fiends themselves and loved nothing more than a ramble through the bush, questing ahead of Luke but checking regularly to ensure he followed.

Luke had kept his word and ordered them to guard her as a friend. They treated her with distant affection, but she knew they would put their lives on the line for her if she was threatened.

She watched them rocket out of the door ahead of Luke. They were soon lost among the rainforest.

Sighing, she turned back to the computer, burying more disturbing thoughts in her favourite therapy— hard work.

She started as hands cupped her eyes from behind. 'Surprise!'

The hands were removed and her chair spun around. 'Kitty! When did you get here?'

Her friend grinned. 'A short time ago. I've been talking to Glen outside. I didn't want to disturb you until you looked interruptible.'

Sarah had just finished making back-up disks of the afternoon's work. She sat back, easing her cramped muscles with one hand. 'How's the photo library business?'

'Great. I'm supplying two hundred stills for a coffee-table book about the Lamington Plateau.'

Sarah thought for a moment. Where was Kitty up to in her alphabetical man-hunt? Then she had it. 'And how are things with you and Kevin?'

Kitty looked uncomfortable. 'We're good friends, so it looks as if I'm going to be stuck on K for a while. What about you?'

'Still footloose and fancy-free,' Sarah told her, with less than total honesty. She and Kitty had had lunch together the day Sarah had collected her things from her flat before moving to Hilltop. Her friend had looked sceptical when Sarah had assured her the move was purely for convenience.

Kitty looked around. 'Where's the gorgeous man himself?'

Sarah shifted uncomfortably. 'Out walking with the dogs. He'll be back in an hour.'

'You should have gone with him. It's a beautiful day.'

'If I had, I'd have missed your visit. So stop looking so—predatory. I told you, I work with Luke. Nothing more.'

'Then why do you turn scarlet at the mention of his name?'

She hadn't, but she did now, thanks to Kitty planting the idea in her mind. 'You're imagining things.' She stood up. 'I'll get us some iced tea and we can talk.'

She came back a few minutes later with the drinks, in tall, frosted glasses, and a plate of Glen's home-made blueberry muffins.

Kitty fumbled in her huge leather satchel. 'I brought your mail and faxes.'

'You're an angel, Kit. Thanks for doing this favour for me.'

'It's worth it to come up and see you, and sample Glen's sensational cooking. Where did Luke find such a treasure?'

'They were at school together in South Australia. Believe it or not, Glen was in the police force but was invalided out after being attacked by a suspect. Glen came to work with Luke on the racing circuit, then stayed around when Luke settled here.'

Kitty let a slow smile develop. 'Sounds like the police force's loss was our gain.'

Sarah favoured her friend with a speculative look. Glen wasn't even the next in alphabetical line, and Kitty was nothing if not a creature of habit. Still, there was no mistaking her interest in Luke's offsider. Well, maybe some good would come of this situation yet.

She flipped through the bundle of letters and faxes. The familiar-looking ones she set aside, along with the junk mail. One fax caught her eye and her breathing quickened as she scanned it. 'Good Lord, I've been invited to host this year's Media Grand Prix at the Mediterranean.'

Kitty looked smug. 'I know; I read the fax. I always knew you had it in you.'

It was the biggest event on the Australian media calendar, when awards were handed out by peer groups to press, television and radio people who'd distinguished themselves in their fields. The 'media Oscars', some people called them.

She frowned at Kitty. 'But why me? I'm not even on the air at present.'

'Doesn't last year's Gold Award winner normally host the current year's event?'

'I only won the Silver for *Coast to Coast*.' It was still a tremendous honour, considerably boosting her status in television journalism.

She read the fax again. 'Of course—Maxine Guy, who *did* win the Gold, now lives in Hollywood. So they've invited me.'

Kitty sipped her tea and bit delicately into a muffin. 'Mmm, these are good. Don't sell yourself short, kiddo. It isn't only because Maxine's overseas. You have talent and the camera loves you.'

'I should be thankful somebody does.' She was unaware of how revealing her comment was until Kitty's eyes narrowed. 'I mean, it's a great honour—especially as I haven't been in front of the camera for nearly a month.'

'Once seen, never forgotten,' Kitty said loyally.

She set her glass down. 'Wait till you tell Luke that you've been chosen.'

Sarah's heart sank. This was precisely the sort of project Luke would find repellent. He would be pleased for her, naturally, but she would read his true reaction in his face before the mask slipped back into place.

He wouldn't hesitate to release her from the book for the week it would take to do the job, allowing for rehearsals, dress fittings, publicity and the actual awards themselves. He would urge her to take whatever time she needed, and all the time she'd be aware of a sense of 'I knew it' lurking in the background. The actual words might never be said, but she'd know they were in his mind.

How long had it taken for her to scurry back to the bright lights? Three weeks? Well, it was probably longer than Luke had expected her to last out here in the wilderness.

She clamped her hands together, aware of a slight tremor. This was the opportunity of a lifetime. Why was she giving Luke's opinion a moment's thought? His manuscript required at most a few months' work. What was she supposed to do when it was finished?

'You don't seem very excited,' Kitty observed between mouthfuls of muffin.

Sarah mustered a smile. 'Naturally, I am. It's just…' She indicated the files spread out around her. 'The writing's going so well.'

Kitty spluttered in amazement. 'You're actually thinking of turning down the Media Grand Prix to work on Luke's book? You're either crazy—or in love with him.'

'Neither, I hope,' she said, aware of speaking a shade too quickly.

Kitty read her like a book. 'It *is* Luke. He'll still be here after the awards, you know.'

Sarah felt bleakness invade her expression. 'I wish I could be sure. He hates all the fanfare that goes with my line of work.'

'But how does he feel about you?'

A shiver of apprehension shook Sarah. She couldn't doubt the answer. The attraction was far from being all on her side. It was in his eyes when he looked at her, and in his touch when he kissed her. She had no doubt that they could become a lot more to each other if things were different.

In spite of the fireworks when they wrote together, they made a good team. In fact much of their success was *due* to the fireworks, because each had a strong point of view and was prepared to defend it. Once one side or the other came up with a convincing argument, they pressed on in complete accord. It meant only the most defensible opinions won out. There were no half-measures.

No half-measures with Luke, either. He was an all-or-nothing man who gave himself to few causes, but those he did he would champion to the hilt. His decision to step out of Formula One racing, once made, had never been questioned. He had never looked back.

'I suspect he feels the same way about me as I feel about him,' Sarah told Kitty with a heavy sigh. 'He's the most dynamic individual I've ever known. He cares about so many things and he doesn't mind showing his emotions.'

'Then what's the problem?'

She gave a wan smile. 'Those emotions run high when it comes to our chosen lifestyles.' She cupped her hands around the frosty tea-glass. 'We're like the people in a weather house—never out at the same time.'

'You really care about him, don't you?'

'These last weeks have been extraordinary. We fight like cat and dog but only about the work. If the fights ever got personal...' She let the thought trail away into silence.

'You can't work it out so he stays home on the farm and you do your thing in public?' Kitty proposed.

Sarah shook her head. 'You know what it would be like. A part-time arrangement, fitted in between ten-hour days at the studio would never suit Luke.'

Kitty inclined her head in understanding. 'I can't see him standing for being called Mr Fox, either.'

Lesser men than Luke had baulked at that, even though women had lived with the deal for centuries. Besides, she'd already been over this ground in her mind and the solution was painfully obvious: do her job and keep her heart out of it. Although she had hoped for a little more time before it came to the crunch.

Crunch-time was here, she accepted, looking at the fax on the couch beside her. Her agent needed an answer right away. She settled her shoulders. 'Of course I'll take the job. You're right; it *is* the chance of a lifetime. Who knows where it will lead?'

She found out only days later, when Luke stormed in carrying the latest copy of the *Gold Coast Herald*.

'Have you seen this?'

His initial reaction to her news had been as she'd predicted: supportive but cool. He was happy for her to abandon the book while she completed the assignment. He had even reminded her that she was a guest at Hilltop, not a prisoner.

He couldn't have been more fair. So why did she have the feeling that she had disappointed him?

She looked at the story in growing dismay. The headline read STARS OUT FOR MEDIA OSCARS. Beneath it was a list of the main nominations and a photo and story about her involvement. The organisers had set it up as soon as she'd agreed to take the job.

What hadn't been anticipated was the photo of Luke alongside hers, with the 'exclusive announcement' that he would escort her to the awards.

'This has to be Richard Nero's doing,' she said. 'No one else would have the nerve. It's his way of retaliating because of what we're doing here.'

'You didn't plant the idea in his head, I suppose?'

Horrified, she stared at him. 'Do you really think me capable of such underhand behaviour?' If he did, there was even less hope for them than she feared.

He gave a sigh of frustration. 'Not really. But it's damned annoying.'

'I'll call my agent and have him set the story straight,' she offered. The damage had been done, but there was little else she could do.

At the same time, a vision of herself at the awards with Luke as her escort was undeniably appealing. 'You wouldn't consider making it true, I suppose?'

His hard look spoke volumes. 'What do you think?'

She sighed. 'I think you'd rather be boiled in oil. I'll call my agent.'

'For all the good it will do,' he threw over his shoulder as he went outside.

He was right, she recognised as she made the call. Even if the paper could be persuaded to print the truth, the retraction would receive far less prominence than the original story.

She paused, the paper in her hand. Their photos did look good side by side. Why on earth was Luke so set against any kind of public exposure? As a world champion five times over, he should be used to finding himself in the news. Yet he hated it with a vehemence bordering on obsession.

His suspicion that she might have planted the story, however quickly he'd withdrawn it, hurt more than she was willing to admit. He evidently didn't know her well enough yet or such a thought would never have crossed his mind.

Her agent held out even less hope that the paper could be persuaded to set the record straight. It occurred to Sarah that her agent might have planted the story himself, to generate more interest in her appearance at the awards banquet.

What was the use? It made little difference who had planted the story. The outcome was the same. The gulf between her and Luke was wider than ever.

It was almost dinner-time, too late to start any new work, if Luke was even interested. She debated whether to take the dogs for a walk on her own, but couldn't summon the enthusiasm. What she really wanted was Luke's company, and he clearly didn't welcome hers.

She found him behind the house, chopping wood for the open fire which dominated the living room. Even at this time of year a fire was occasionally needed during the cool, misty nights. But Luke attacked the logs for another purpose, as if to work off a store of anger. At the newspapers? The world? At her?

The woodpile consisted of massive tree trunks stacked head-high in a mosaic pattern. Most were collected from around the property after storms had blown them over, or were dragged from the ground when they died. Using living trees for fuel wasn't Luke's way.

He was working on a huge eucalyptus log, the axe-head whistling as it tore through the air to take a wedge-shaped bite out of the iron-hard wood. His shirt was open to the waist, the sleeves rolled above his elbows. Sweat ran in rivers down his magnificent body, oiling it to sculpted perfection. Her mouth dried as she looked at him.

It was dangerous work, demanding total concentration. The axe was razor-sharp, a mistimed blow capable of severing a foot. Luke never missed a beat. Time after time the axe flashed upwards, blurring down again to bite into the log until it was sundered into four even-sized pieces.

Luke dropped the axe and threw the cut logs onto a pile ready to be taken inside. The sweet smell of the wood chips mingled with the odour of earth and fallen leaves. It was a fragrance she was unlikely to forget, linked as it always would be with the almost primeval sight she'd just witnessed.

He shouldered the axe and turned, catching sight of her. 'How long have you been there?'

She folded her arms. 'Long enough to guess they weren't really logs you were hacking into.'

He looked wary, as if caught out at something. 'What are you getting at?'

'Who were you punishing, Luke? Me?'

He rested the axe against a tree. 'God, no. I accept your word you had nothing to do with the story.'

'Then who?'

'Leave it, can't you?' The words came at her through gritted teeth.

But she'd had enough of mysteries. 'No, I won't. Either you tell me what this is really about or—or—I'll call the paper and tell them you're not only escorting me to the awards but we're sleeping together as well.'

He moved nearer to her, forcing her to retreat towards the woodpile. 'I could make it true.'

'Which one?' she asked, with a bravado she was far from feeling. The anger in Luke's eyes warned her that any passion which flared between them now would have more to do with revenge than love.

She kept her head high, refusing to let him see the torrent of emotions ravening through her. After a moment he turned aside, swearing under his breath. 'Very well. You wanted to know it all. How would you feel if the media accused you of killing your fiancée and unborn child—and the worst of it was, they could be right?'

Horror washed through her. It couldn't be true.

One look at his haggard expression told her he believed it was.

'What happened?' she asked in a tortured undertone.

He dragged in a lungful of air, resting a hand against the woodpile as he started to speak. 'Kathy worked with the promoters on the Formula One circuit. We met, dated, fell in love—the usual story. We were to be married in Europe at the close of the racing season.'

His matter-of-fact tone heightened rather than disguised the pain of his memories. Sarah hardly dared breathe for fear of driving him back into his shell. He was Prometheus, chained to the rock of his tragedy. She prayed that sharing it with her could help him break the chains and scatter the vultures.

What it might do to her, she didn't dare to consider.

'In Europe I was considered the playboy of the racing circuit,' he went on in the same flat tone. But his white-knuckle grip on a log didn't escape her notice. 'I raced hard, played hard, drank hard. I was what you would call "good copy". Your media cohorts didn't like it when I got engaged and showed every sign of settling down. They kept raking up past transgressions and speculating on how long my engagement would last.'

It was typical gutter journalism, and Sarah had seen plenty of it in her career. 'So what did you do?'

'Resisted the urge to punch out every photographer who followed us around. They were waiting for me to pull some such stunt because it sold more papers.'

She nodded in understanding. 'It can't have been easy.'

He laughed harshly. 'You don't know the half of it. The irony was, all the attention meant that a kidnapper was able to track Kathy's movements and make a grab for her when she was on the way to a meeting with me.'

She couldn't restrain her gasp of dismay. 'Oh, Luke.'

His eyes were flame. 'I saw her being bundled into a car and took off after them. They eventually plunged their car off the same road where Grace Kelly was killed. There were no survivors.'

Sarah's eyes were puzzled. 'But you said *you* were accused of killing your fiancée.'

'According to the press, I was a glory-seeker who had forced the kidnapper to drive recklessly by following him at high speed instead of trying to negotiate.'

'But surely you called the police first?'

'I tried, but my carphone wasn't working. Something was jamming it. At least it was at first. Later, when the police tested it, it worked perfectly. So maybe the press was right. Maybe I *did* cause Kathy's death by trying to be a hero.'

'You don't really believe that?'

'When the headlines call you a killer, it's hard to argue.'

'And you think it will happen again when the unauthorised biography comes out?'

His gaze hardened. 'It makes better copy than the truth, which was that something was jamming my phone and I had no choice but to try to keep the kidnapper's car in sight.'

He raked strong fingers through his hair. 'The irony

is, I followed them quite slowly, not wanting to get too close and spook them into doing anything reckless. I only speeded up when I saw them lose control and go over the cliff. But it was too late.'

She guessed the rest. 'And the police found your skidmarks at the scene and concluded you were in a high-speed chase.'

He nodded. 'All the evidence pointed to it, including my track record. For a long time I even wondered if they were right. If I *had* waited for the police, would Kathy still be alive?'

Sarah placed a hand on his arm. 'You did what you had to at the time. The journalists weren't there. They had no right to judge you.'

He raised bleak eyes to her. 'I didn't even discover she was pregnant until after she died.'

A pang gripped Sarah. He had lost so much, and the media hadn't helped by making him blame himself. No wonder he had little time for the members of her profession. They had put him through a hell no man should have to suffer. And now it was in danger of happening all over again, when the unauthorised book came out.

'I'm sorry. I didn't know,' she said. If only she'd continued her research into his background, she might have been better prepared for this.

'You probably would have read about it here, but in the days following the crash there was a wave of terrorist bomb threats at airports around Australia, and my story was relegated to a couple of paragraphs in the sports pages. Otherwise I've no doubt your colleagues would have had a field-day, as they did in Europe.'

Her heart bled for him, even as she recognised the hopelessness of their situation. She belonged to the group which had hounded him throughout his tragedy, publicly holding him responsible for the deaths of his fiancée and his unborn child. Every step she'd taken since he pulled her from the wreckage of her car had been another nail in the coffin of their relationship. Short of giving up everything she'd ever worked for, she could never be the woman for him.

But true love was giving, and there was still a way to show him that her kind weren't all the same. Her voice was husky as she said, 'Thank you for telling me, Luke. I wish there was something I could do to make it easier for you.'

As she turned away he asked harshly, 'Where are you going?'

She could hardly speak for the emotions churning through her. 'Inside. I have a phone call to make.'

CHAPTER EIGHT

FOR long seconds after Sarah went inside, Luke stayed where he was, mastering his turbulent emotions. Damn the woman. She had an amazing ability to turn him inside out. He hadn't intended to tell her so much about his history, but with Sarah he found himself wanting to share parts of himself he normally didn't reveal to anyone.

He wasn't even sure what was behind it. He wanted her with him more than he had ever wanted any woman. Thanks to what she'd just learned, she sounded as if she was about to agree. So why wasn't he turning handsprings? Instead he felt as if he'd just committed a terrible crime.

He recognised the source of the feeling. Because it wasn't right for her. The realisation hit him as if he'd been struck by his own axe. He had plenty of reason for burying himself here in the backwoods, but Sarah had real talent and the ambition to reach the top in her field. He had no right to give in to his own desires and encourage her to stay. It was too much to ask.

It was almost too much *not* to ask.

But he couldn't do it to her. She deserved much better and he intended to see that she got it, no matter what the cost to himself. Still, it was all he could do to make his legs move and follow her inside.

Sarah braced herself for a storm after she told her agent what she had decided. It wasn't long in coming.

'What do you mean, you won't appear at the Media Grand Prix? Are you ill? Or only taken leave of your senses?'

All of the above, where Luke was concerned. She didn't expect her agent to understand but she tried anyway. 'I think I'm finally *coming* to my senses, Phil.'

There was a long pause during which she pictured the man wrestling with his temper. In the industry, Phil was known for his short fuse. It was a miracle he was being this patient with her.

'Is it because of the article about you and Luke Ansfield?' he asked finally. 'I'll get a retraction printed. We'll tell them you can't stand the man.'

She took a steadying breath. 'I'd appreciate the retraction, but not at Luke's expense.' In any case, it was far from the truth. But she didn't say so to Phil.

'You haven't done anything stupid like fall for him, have you? The man's a hermit.' Another long silence, then, 'Saints preserve us, you *have* joined the hermitage. I knew when you started writing this book it would mean trouble.'

Confusion made Sarah's voice unsteady. By committing herself to Luke she was saying no to a future she had always believed she wanted more than anything. Had she really changed that much in such a short time? She felt the answer to the depths of her soul. 'Being a hermit isn't so bad, Phil,' she assured her agent.

'You can't mean it,' Phil coaxed. 'This job is a dream come true for you. At least admit that much?'

'I admit it is a dream job,' she agreed heavily, unable to deny that she was giving up a great deal. Her voice sounded wistful even to her own ears. 'But my mind is made up.' And it was, she accepted with a rush of certainty. Luke meant more to her than any spotlight ever could.

Phil talked on and she heard herself agreeing that, yes, it was the chance of a lifetime, and yes, she was a fool to turn it down. But all the time her heart sang an inner song of rightness she could never hope to communicate to him. 'Promise me you'll sleep on your decision,' Phil said at last. 'By tomorrow you'll see things differently. Call me then.'

He wasn't going to give up until she agreed. 'Okay, I'll sleep on it and call you tomorrow,' she said on a deep sigh, 'but my decision will be the same.'

Slowly she replaced the receiver, and only then became aware of Luke looming in the doorway. Her heart leapt at the sight of him. If he had monitored the conversation, then he knew she had made her choice. 'You heard?'

He nodded tautly, looking far less happy than she'd expected. 'I heard.'

In truth he had heard a lot more than Sarah realised, he thought. He hadn't missed the wistfulness in her voice as she walked away from a career which meant so much to her. Thank goodness he had also heard her agent persuade her to sleep on her decision, giving Luke the chance to change her mind.

He could think of only one way to do it. 'Tomorrow you're going to call your agent and tell him you've thought it over and you *will* appear at those awards.'

She looked confused. 'You mean you want me to do it?'

He shook his head. 'What I want doesn't enter into it. I won't let you commit professional suicide over nothing more than a fantasy.'

She looked as if someone had struck her, and his resolution almost wavered—until he reminded himself that her future happiness was what mattered. 'I thought you'd be pleased about my decision. Now you're saying it's a fantasy?' How could the attraction between them be anything but real?

He spread his hands wide, palms down. 'It probably always was a fantasy. It just took me some time to see it. You were right all along. We're too different. Now it's time we faced facts and got on with our separate lives.'

She felt numb with shock and pain. She had finally admitted to herself that she wanted to be with Luke more than she wanted any professional assignment on offer. Now he was telling her that it was a wasted sacrifice, one he didn't even welcome. It was almost too much to take in.

She had been so sure that she was making the right choice, turning down this job to show him how committed she was to their future, and how different she was from the colleagues who had caused him so much anguish.

Her sacrifice would never bring back his fiancée and unborn child, but it was something she wanted to do to give them a chance at a future together. Now he was telling her it wasn't enough, that they had no future no matter what she did. Could it be true that the attraction was only strong while she remained out of his reach? It was the only explanation which made any sense to her confused mind.

Luke's dark eyes bored almost to her soul. 'I have a fair idea what this is all about, and it's precisely why I didn't tell you everything sooner. You have talent, Sarah. You're destined for better things than burying yourself in a rainforest hide-away with me. I won't let you throw away your future to no good purpose.'

His words rang through her like hammer-blows. He was determined to send her away, labelling her feelings a fantasy. He began to pace, his face rigidly expressionless. It came to her that this was the man who had controlled mighty racing machines of unimaginable power over some of the most demanding circuits in the world. What hope did she have of altering his course so much as a millimetre once his mind was made up?

If he didn't care for her, was there any point in trying?

'Think about this,' he went on urgently. 'Every important member of your industry will attend those awards. You'll be the host of the night and every eye will be on you. It could open doors you can't begin to imagine.'

The truth had to come out. 'Maybe it isn't what I want any more.'

'It damned well better be.' The harsh, grating statement stabbed through her with almost physical impact. 'Because it's your life, Sarah. Not this backwoods existence. There's no future for you here, however much you think you want it now. How long until it becomes a prison of all your hopes and dreams? The place where your ambition died? Do you think I'd allow such a thing?'

A tiny flame of hope flickered inside her. If he cared enough to drive her away for her own sake, maybe there was a future for them, after all.

He read the hope and moved to extinguish it with a savage cutting gesture. 'Whatever you're fantasising about, forget it. You aren't Cinderella and I'm not the Prince, offering you a happy ever after. We're business associates, working together on a book, and maybe that was a mistake if it gave you the wrong idea about me.'

She refused to let him see how deeply his words wounded her. She wasn't even sure she believed them. Luke was a master at hiding his feelings. How could she be sure he wasn't hiding them now, to ensure she took the opportunity offered to her?

'Very well,' she said, more calmly than she felt, 'but if I got the wrong idea about us, you contributed to it when you kissed me.'

She locked eyes with him, not letting him forget what had passed between them in the cavern beneath the ancient fig tree. Let him explain *that* away as a misunderstanding on her part.

He didn't even try. 'It doesn't change the facts. You don't belong here.' His look blazed into her. 'How long would it be before you got sick of what Hilltop had to offer—what I have to offer—and went anyway?'

Sudden understanding bloomed within her. '*That's* what this is all about? You want rid of me sooner rather than later because you think it's inevitable? My God, Luke, I thought you were coming to know me.'

'Perhaps better than you know yourself,' he observed in a low voice.

Stopped in her tracks, she could only stare at him. She didn't believe she would change her mind about preferring Luke's lifestyle to her own, but how could she know after only a few weeks' working with him? How did it compare with ambition instilled into her over a lifetime? She didn't want to own that he could be right, but she had to acknowledge at least the possibility.

Still she had to try once more. 'Do you want me to leave?'

In tense silence she awaited his answer. No hint of his feelings was visible on his face, which was a stone mask, but there was a bleakness in the sea-dark eyes which made her ache for him.

'You *are* leaving,' he said, avoiding her original question. 'You'll host the awards ceremony and you'll be brilliant at it. Then you'll forget you had anything to do with me.'

She might do the first two but she was unlikely to do the last, not for a very long time.

Pride wouldn't allow her to beg him to change his mind. All that remained was to walk away with her head high. 'What will you do about the book?' she asked in a parting shot which refused to recognise that it could possibly be over.

He smiled bitterly. 'What I should have done from the beginning—written it myself without involving anyone else.'

So hurt she could barely see for the blurring in her vision, she blinked rapidly to clear it. If he needed her at all, he was doing an amazing job of disguising the fact. Hard to believe he meant anything but what he said. 'All right, Luke,' she said on a note of resignation, 'I'll go back to my life as ordered. But you can't order me to forget you—and I don't believe you can forget me.'

An eyebrow canted upwards. 'More wishful thinking?'

'There's a way to find out. Kiss me again and show me how little it means to you.'

For the first time she saw a tiny crack in the stone façade. 'What's the point?'

She kept her gaze steady although her heart was pounding. 'I think you know, but if you're afraid...'

Before she could complete the taunt she was swept into an iron-hard embrace which drove most of the air from her body.

Luke's arms were like bands of steel around her. With all the power and passion at his command, he claimed her mouth in a kiss which set her senses spinning.

He wanted to arouse her. She understood that in the distant part of her mind which still retained any semblance of control. He wanted to prove that what they had shared was simple chemistry, nothing more.

He was dangerously close to succeeding. As he explored her mouth, his body aligned with hers, she was aware of every hard contour, every inch of padded muscle. Her own body sang a siren song of response, moulding to him in a way which she would have found slightly shocking if it hadn't felt so profoundly right.

She was overwhelmed by the need to feel, to taste, to be with him, despite knowing there was no future for them as long as he insisted on nobly letting her go. She was rapidly tiring of nobility when it denied her—this. Into her response she poured all her frustrations, all her yearnings, all her hopes for what could never be.

She felt his reluctance to release her mastered by some tough, masculine core of purpose. Yet when he put her away from him his expression was shell-shocked. She glimpsed it only for a minute, a look filled with such raw pain and need that it shook her to the core.

Then the shuttered look returned and he was in command again. 'Is that what you wanted?' he rasped.

What she wanted was some hope that they could work this out, somehow carve a future out of a past blighted by his tragedy. She shook her head. 'It wasn't what I wanted, but it will have to serve because it's all I'm ever going to have, isn't it?'

Not waiting for an answer, she shouldered past him, holding onto control with every bit of professional training she had.

It wasn't in her to beg any man to love her, but she was dangerously close to doing it now. The sooner she got out of here, and on with her life, the better.

It would serve Luke right if she soared to such dizzy heights that he would need to make an appointment to see her ever again.

CHAPTER NINE

IT FELT odd to be living in her own apartment again, although she'd been away for longer periods on assignments for *Coast to Coast*. It wasn't the length of time, Sarah recognised, so much as the intensity of her stay with Luke making her feel like a stranger in her own home.

She was busy enough. Getting ready for the awards ceremony involved fittings for a spectacular gown, rehearsals and advance publicity. If not for the endless nights, she might have convinced herself she didn't miss Luke at all.

'Have you heard from him?' Kitty asked after arriving unannounced during a lull in Sarah's frantic schedule. She came armed with barbecued chicken, salads, and rolls fresh from the bakery, disdainfully pushing aside the tub of yoghurt which would have been Sarah's meal.

Sarah dropped onto a stool, belatedly accepting how tired she was. She appreciated Kitty's thoughtfulness, but her appetite had deserted her lately.

She picked at the plate of chicken and salad in front of her. 'Luke hasn't called and I don't expect him to,' she said on what she hoped was a note of finality.

She might have known Kitty wouldn't take the hint. 'Have you called him?'

'Yes. I—wanted to see how the book was going.' It was the excuse she'd given herself when she'd picked up the phone. But either Luke hadn't been at home or Glen had been given instructions not to put her calls through, because she'd made no progress.

As it was, hearing Glen's voice had almost been her undoing. Without a rehearsal to attend, she would have been tempted to drive up to Hilltop and see Luke.

And say what? He'd already made his feelings clear by sending her away. She might feel like Cinderella, ballgown and all at the ready, but if the Prince didn't want to play his role, the fairytale was over.

Which was precisely Luke's point, wasn't it?

She came back to her surroundings with a jolt as Kitty snapped two fingers in front of her face. 'Come back to me, Sarah. If you don't want to eat any more, how about showing me the gown I've heard so much about.'

Sarah managed a wan smile. 'So that's what this visit is all about. You realise what I'm wearing is supposed to be a secret until the night of the awards?'

Kitty passed an index finger across her mouth. 'My lips are sealed.'

Why couldn't her real sisters be more like Kitty? Sarah wondered as she went to fetch the gown. Between her and Kitty there was no competitiveness. They could tell each other anything.

Or they had been able to until now, she thought, lifting the gown out of its nest of tissue. She hadn't been able to tell her friend how she felt about Luke. It was all she could do to be honest with herself.

But Kitty was ahead of her as usual. She gasped in appreciation when Sarah modelled the Aloys Gada original.

It was a stunning fantasy dress of crushed-strawberry crystal organza encrusted with jewels, the pleated bustier-style bodice falling to a slim skirt and full organza over-skirt. Matching Thai silk shoes with Louis heels and jewelled toes completed the outfit.

'It's incredible; you look like royalty,' Kitty said on a sigh, then frowned. 'But something's not right.'

Sarah spun towards the mirrored wall in the dining room but could see no flaw in the magnificent dress. 'With the gown?'

Kitty shook her head. 'With the wearer.'

Sarah's stance telegraphed her surprise. 'What do you mean?'

'Oh, Sarah, you're not exactly a picture of radiance. If anything, the gown makes you look more fragile than usual. As if you were pining for something—or someone.'

Sarah plucked at the crisp folds of the over-skirt. 'You're imagining things, Kit.'

'Am I imagining your pallor? The fact that you're eating like a bird—and your sudden interest in reading back issues of *Chequered Flag*?'

The incriminating Formula One racing magazines still lay on the coffee-table. Sarah let her shoulders drop. 'All right, I was reading up on Luke's history, but it isn't going to change reality. He doesn't want my lifestyle and won't allow me to share his.'

She drew herself up, fanning the gown around her as if it would provide a bulwark against her inner turmoil. 'So I'm getting on with my life.'

Kitty sighed. 'Even if it kills you?'

'Despite what the books and films tell you, nobody dies of unrequited passion.'

Doubt and admiration chased each other across Kitty's open features. 'I'm relieved to hear it, because my cinematographer, Kevin, has friends in high places at your old studio. Word is your former partner, Richard Nero, is slipping badly in the ratings. Since you left, *Coast to Coast* has lost its sparkle—and I'm not saying it because you're my friend. It's the simple truth.'

Sarah stared at her friend in surprise. Since going to work with Luke, Sarah hadn't given her old programme a moment's thought. Becoming the show's permanent anchor had meant everything to her less than a month ago. What had happened?

Luke had happened, she acknowledged to herself. Without saying a word, he'd shown her the futility of blind ambition. Succeeding to satisfy her parents or impress her sisters would never be enough for her now. It was up to her to find her own star and follow it to the best of her ability.

'What will you do if they offer you the show?' Kitty asked into the deepening silence.

Sarah looked at Kitty carefully. 'Probably turn it down.'

Kitty's gasp hissed between them. 'To do what?'

'Write,' Sarah said slowly, knowing that the idea had been growing on her for some time. 'I loved working with Luke on the book. Watching the manuscript pages pile up was the biggest buzz I've had in ages. I'd like to write a book on my own, maybe a novel with a television background.'

Kitty grinned wickedly. 'They say you should write what you know. You could do an exposé of the industry.'

'Maybe not an exposé, but a racy, pacy page-turner,' Sarah said, warming to the concept. 'The kind where you try and guess who the characters are based on.'

Kitty lifted a glass of mineral water in a toast. 'Go for it, Sarah. Then watch how fast your racing driver comes running, when he realises he's let such a catch get away.'

Kitty was wrong. Any success she attained as a writer wouldn't bring Luke to heel. If anything it would drive him further away. After his tragic experience with the media, he wasn't interested in someone with her background.

He thought leopards couldn't change their spots, and maybe he was right. Planning a career as a best-selling novelist hardly qualified as fading into the background.

Was he right in saying she couldn't live in obscurity? Since he wasn't about to give her the chance, she was unlikely to find out.

Obscurity was the least of her problems over the next few days. As the night of the media awards drew closer she was caught up in a whirlwind of interviews and photographs as everybody speculated about the likely winners.

Predictably, her parents adored having her at the centre of it all. Tickets to the event were as precious as gold but she'd obtained good seats for them, which made her even more popular. Once she would have revelled in their praise, but now it seemed hardly to matter.

Even when her sister, Isabel, telephoned from

Canberra to gossip about the nominees from the parliamentary press corps, Sarah was unmoved. She would have preferred Isabel to ring simply to catch up with her sister.

What would her family say when they found out she meant to abandon all this for a precarious career as a novelist? She liked to think they'd be supportive, but either way it wouldn't change her decision.

The real problem was Luke, she told herself as she allowed herself to be gowned and coiffed for the big event in a hotel suite adjacent to the banquet hall. In a fit of misplaced optimism she'd sent him a ticket to the dinner, but she didn't expect him to attend. She wanted him to, she recognised. But she didn't really expect him to spend an entire evening rubbing shoulders with people he hated, merely for her sake.

Adding fuel to Luke's dislike of the media, they were still speculating in print about his possible relationship with Sarah. Well, they would find out the truth when he didn't show up tonight, she thought bleakly.

'Nervous?' her dresser asked.

'A little.' More like downhearted, but she didn't say so. She couldn't help thinking about the empty chair at the official table. She made an effort to smile and thank her helpers as they finished their work and left her finally, blessedly alone, to compose herself before showtime.

A knock at the door of the suite made her heart sink. She really needed these few moments to herself. But it might be important so, squaring her shoulders, she went to answer it. The artificial smile she'd pasted to her lips faded as she saw who stood there.

'Luke,' she said in a tortured whisper. 'What are you doing here?'

'You invited me to escort you to the dinner,' he reminded her.

Her face told him she hadn't really expected him to come. Now he was here and she drank in the sight of him in stunned silence.

He looked marvellous, resplendent in a black three-button dinner jacket with silk shawl collar, a black brocade waistcoat, emphasising his muscular build, and black trousers creased to a knife-edge.

His skin glowed beneath a white piqué wing-collared shirt. He looked a little tired, too, she noted, with the odd awareness she seemed to have developed around him. There were telltale lines around his eyes she couldn't recall seeing before, and his generous mouth seemed drawn.

He was still incredibly attractive. As he surveyed her in the stunning gown his eyes glittered like chips of diamond. A muscle worked along his jawline. 'You look lovely, Sarah.'

Her throat dried. 'Thank you.' So do you, she wanted to add, but the moment felt fragile, as if she could destroy it by saying too much. Instead, she looked her fill. Her nervousness had vanished. With Luke at her side she could take on the world.

Except for one problem. 'You know what tonight will mean? TV cameras, reporters—all the things you dislike the most.'

He shook his head. 'Not everything. You were right about one thing, Sarah, you did have an effect on me. I can't let you give up your future on my account, but neither can I let you do this alone.'

The silken texture of his voice was seductive, yet warning bells shrilled through her. He was here for tonight only, no more. His feelings hadn't changed. Only his sense of justice had brought him to her side.

She found her voice with an effort. 'You don't have to put yourself through this as a favour to me.'

'It's no favour. I want to be here.'

She found herself smiling. Why not simply enjoy the gift of this night? Luke wanted to be here. It was nothing compared to the way she wanted him at her side, but she intended to enjoy every golden moment.

At some level there existed the risk of heartbreak tomorrow, but she wouldn't think of it tonight. Eat, drink and be merry, she told herself recklessly as she took the arm he offered and stepped out into the glare of spotlights.

The ballroom decorations echoed the heyday of the British Raj in India, with canopied ceiling, silk-lined walls, tables decorated with scarlet bougainvillea, and a trickling fountain as a centrepiece. Blue Venetian glass chandeliers turned the sparkle of candles into a starfield of flickering lights.

The ceremony was to be televised nationally, followed by a banquet then dancing until dawn, when the participants could let their hair down out of sight of the television cameras.

Sarah felt as if she was walking on air. The ceremony went like a dream. Not once did the autocue fail to deliver her lines, none of the celebrity presenters drank to excess, at least not until they'd done their jobs, and the winners kept their acceptance speeches mercifully short. Some were even witty.

Every time Sarah needed a fresh charge of adrena-

lin all she had to do was let her eye fall on Luke,
seated at the official table immediately below her lec-
tern. Knowing what an ordeal this must be for him,
she was impressed by his coolness as he dealt with
the attention lavished on him by the cameras.

Despite his long absence from the public eye, he
had been recognised and applauded as he escorted
Sarah to the stage. A resourceful technician had
flashed Luke's name up as a subtitle for the viewers
at home. The anonymity he cherished was fast becoming a memory.

He didn't seem to mind, although she was sure
much of it was an act for her benefit. Part of her ached
for what he was giving up for her sake, but she
couldn't bring herself to regret a moment. This was
her night, and by his presence Luke had given her the
greatest gift he could.

It came to her that this was part of his intention—
to enhance her professional image. She'd be so much
in demand in her own world he'd have no qualms
about his decision. It was a galling thought, but why
else would he put himself through such an ordeal?

The thought that this was his last gift to her almost
undermined her composure. It took every ounce of
professionalism she could muster to sail through the
remainder of the broadcast as if nothing was amiss.

The compliments thrust upon her as she came off-
stage told her it had worked. Now she had only to
survive the banquet with her pride intact.

Luke stood up as she returned to their table. 'You
were magnificent. Congratulations.'

She mustered a smile but didn't take the chair he
offered. 'Thank you. I'm going out onto the terrace

for some air.' Anything to avoid sitting beside him, knowing it was probably for the last time.

He forestalled her. 'I'll join you.'

She was achingly aware of him as they threaded their way between the tables, but thankfully there was no opportunity for a personal moment.

With the broadcast over, people table-hopped enthusiastically. Their progress was slow across the room as Sarah fielded congratulations and well-wishers.

They were not the only people seeking fresh air, she found when they reached the terrace. Her former producer from *Coast to Coast*, Donna Blake, was already there with her date.

Her face lit up when she saw Sarah. 'Darling, you were marvellous tonight.'

Accepting the air kisses Donna bestowed on her, Sarah looked around. 'Richard not with you?'

Donna shook her head. 'It isn't official yet, but his last show went to air this evening.'

Thanks to Kitty, Sarah already knew that *Coast to Coast* wasn't rating well, but this news came as a shock. She felt Luke's hand tighten on her arm. She could practically hear his thoughts: play your cards right and the job could be yours.

She drew a steadying breath, trying to still the fast beating of her heart which had nothing to do with Donna's news and everything to do with Luke's touch. It was all she could do not to lean back into the comforting curve of his arm.

She made an effort to straighten. 'I'm sorry about Richard. Who'll be taking over the show?'

Donna looked smug. 'The weekend anchor is filling in for now. You and I need to talk, Sarah.'

It wouldn't do any good because Sarah's mind was already made up. But she would rather tell Donna when Luke wasn't with her, to avoid letting him think this was anything but her own idea. 'Call me,' she said non-committally.

Donna seemed satisfied. 'I see you two are still an item,' she said, her wide smile including Luke. 'How's the book going?'

'Almost completed,' he told her, obviously not inclined to tell Donna the real state of affairs. Sarah was foolishly glad. The truth couldn't be avoided for long, but she would rather not fuel gossip in an industry which thrived on it.

She fell silent, unwillingly fascinated by the way Luke wove his charm around Donna. The producer practically purred, neglecting her own date to bask in Luke's attention. After a time, she pried herself away with obvious reluctance.

'How did I do?' Luke asked into Sarah's ear when they were alone again.

'You should have been an agent,' she snapped, pain making her voice sharp. 'Why don't you put a price sticker on my forehead and be done with it?'

His eyebrow arched upwards. 'You lost your big chance once over me. The least I can do is make sure it doesn't happen again.'

He was so sure this was where she belonged; it never occurred to him that she might have changed. She tensed as his hand slid across the small of her back. 'I care about you, Sarah. I want you to be happy.'

'And out of your hair,' she said flatly, acknowledging the bitter truth. Never mind if her body refused to accept it, her mind had to. The wanting which dragged through her so insistently had to be silenced.

Or given in to.

For one wild, fantastic moment she imagined assuaging that desperate longing by letting him make love to her. No matter what else he commanded, she was certain of her power in this. She could enthral him with her female wiles until he had no choice but to share himself with her.

Her heart raced at the thought of taking him within her, shaping herself to his driving passions even as she answered him with her own.

Her breathing quickened and a surge of heat tore through her from head to foot. It was no answer. Whoever said you should deal with temptation by giving in to it should have added, over and over again. She had no doubt that with Luke once would be too often...and never enough.

Her movements were stiff, her entire being screaming a protest as she made herself leave the circle of his arms. 'Come inside and meet my parents.'

Like Donna, Sarah's mother and father were captivated by Luke's natural charm. To her mother he showed a genuine interest in the doings of all her daughters—the one sure way to her heart—and with Sarah's father he exchanged views on the power of the media—very much her father's hobby-horse.

Yet Sarah had no sense that Luke was deliberately being all things to all people. Heaven knew, she'd seen enough of that in the television industry, where it was frequently a case of, 'Enough about me, let's talk about you—what do you think of me?'

Luke's interest was too genuine to be faked. He enjoyed crossing verbal swords with her father, she noted in surprise. It gave her a new insight into her parents as well, enabling her to see them as interesting people in their own right.

Her mother drew her aside. 'I want you to know how proud we are of you, Sarah.'

She raised her head. 'Because of tonight?'

'Because of all your achievements. Look at the way people regard you. Sometimes, I wish...' She trailed off, chewing her lower lip.

Wondering what was coming, Sarah said, 'Go on.'

'I wish your sisters were more like you,' her mother confided. 'Leanne is so flighty, and Isabel changes her opinions to suit the way the political wind's blowing. But you've always known your own mind and stuck to your guns.'

Sarah felt her jaw dropping and covered her shock with a smile, impulsively enveloping her mother in a hug. 'I love you, Mum,' she said, and meant it.

Later she would need time to work out how she felt about this news. For now, it felt wonderful. She wasn't the failed daughter, after all. Without knowing it, her mother's vote of confidence had set the seal on her plans for the future. They would be proud of her no matter what she did or didn't do.

If only Luke felt the same, everything would be perfect.

But Sarah was under no illusions. This ball would end at midnight, with Cinderella having to leave. There would be no prince searching for her, glass slipper in hand. Some of her joy evaporated as she faced facts. The prospect of going on without Luke weighed heavily on her heart. He had filled places within her she hadn't even known were empty.

Now they would never be filled, because he wouldn't allow himself to love her. Instead he was forcing her out of his life, to live the fairytale existence he thought was right for her, when the truth was that life with him was the only life she wanted.

Whatever her mother said next was lost in the stark realisation which came to her with all the force of a wave crashing against the shore.

She was in love with Luke.

Why hadn't she seen it before? This fierce wanting which threatened to consume her wasn't sexual attraction. That was part of it, naturally, and the very thought made her catch fire, but there was so much more. And it added up to a love she'd hidden even from herself until now.

It would have to stay hidden, especially from Luke. He didn't want her and most certainly didn't love her. She owed it to herself to walk away with her head high, pretending that he was right and her career was all that mattered.

'Like to dance?' he asked when her parents took their leave. They had enjoyed themselves, they assured her, but it was late and they had a long drive home.

Sarah wished she could leave with them. Dancing with Luke was foolishly risky. He was a clever judge of people. It would take considerable acting skill to keep him from sensing her true feelings.

But a refusal would be even more of a give-away,

so she followed him onto the dance floor and tried desperately to relax as he took her into his arms.

The music was slow and sensuous, or maybe it was in her head, because, despite her best efforts to remain aloof, she felt heat spreading through her at his touch.

His fluid steps brought them close together until she could feel his warmth radiating through his evening clothes. One hand rested low on her back, the other cradled her close, his breath whispering against her heated cheeks.

Confusion made her miss a step and his hold tightened. 'Are you okay? Not too tired?'

'Not at all,' she answered, feeling her heart almost stop. It was the excuse she craved, yet she didn't take advantage of it. She had only to agree that yes, she was tired, and they could return to their table, perhaps end the evening altogether.

What was the matter with her? He didn't love her so why didn't she end this now, before any more damage was done?

In just a few seconds she would, she promised herself. She was storing up memories, the way a squirrel hoarded food against a hard winter. That the winter would be a long one, perhaps never-ending, she refused to consider.

Nevertheless, she was far from ready when the music ended to polite applause. Before they could return to the table, they were approached by an attendant. 'Excuse me, Mr Ansfield, you're wanted on the phone urgently.'

Questions buzzed in her brain as she followed Luke to a screened courtesy-phone, mobile phones having been left at the entrance by request. It wouldn't have done to have a ringing telephone interrupt the broadcast.

The call was brief, Luke's answers terse. Something was wrong, she gathered.

'What is it?' she asked when he ended the call.

A frown cut a deep V in his forehead. 'It was Glen. There's been a break-in at Hilltop.'

'But the dogs...'

'Drugged,' he said shortly. 'I have to get back right away. I'll drop you at home on my way.'

She shook her head. 'There's no need.'

He mastered his frustration with an obvious effort. 'Then how will you get home? By cab?'

'I'm not going home,' she said, reaching a decision. Resolutions were made to be broken. She had vowed to walk away tonight, but that had been before this happened. Before she knew he was going to need her. Afterwards might be a different matter, but for now she knew what she had to do. 'I'm coming to Hilltop with you.'

He swore softly. 'The hell you are.'

She lifted her head, her eyes meeting his unflinchingly. 'The hell I am. You can take me with you or I can follow in my own car.'

He took a split-second to decide. 'You'll be safer in my car, where I can keep an eye on you. Let's go.'

CHAPTER TEN

SHE must be crazy, Sarah told herself. What on earth had possessed her to accompany Luke back to Hilltop? He didn't want her with him and he'd have his hands full dealing with the break-in. So why was she sitting beside him in his car, her fabulous designer gown crushed around her, as they streaked through the dark streets towards the highway?

He didn't need her. She would probably be in the way. But no power on earth could have prevented her from coming with him, least of all Luke himself.

'Scenting a story, Sarah?' he asked, his eyes fixed on the road ahead. Not surprisingly, he handled the car with consummate skill, his long-fingered hands resting easily on the steering wheel as he powered the car around each turn.

His comment, made so casually, stabbed through her. She could feel the tension winding between them but hadn't expected him to make such an assumption.

'I didn't insist on coming out of professional curiosity,' she said carefully.

'Why not? It would be quite a scoop for the new anchor on *Coast to Coast*.'

'I haven't agreed to take the job yet,' she reminded him. 'Even if I did, I wouldn't use my friends to get stories.'

He dragged in an audible breath. 'Of course not. It came out without thinking. Of all people, I should know better than to doubt your sense of honour. You kept quiet about me when it could have gained you the centre seat much sooner.'

She felt chilled, blamed it on the car's efficient air-conditioning system. 'Thank you for the belated vote of confidence.'

He raked a hand through his hair, the silver streaks gleaming in the moonlight. 'All right, I'm sorry for even giving the idea house-room.'

How could she stay angry with him when he sounded so desperately worried? 'It's the break-in, I know,' she said, banishing her own hurt feelings. Later would be soon enough to examine them. She focused on Luke's problem. 'You said Glen was all right?' she said. His assistant's wellbeing had been Luke's first concern.

'Thankfully. He was out of the house when the thieves got in. There was a small brush-fire at the back of the property and Glen had gone to attend to it.'

Luke sounded so raw that Sarah wished there was some way she could help him. She knew what was wrong, of course. He blamed himself for accepting her invitation to the awards banquet. If he hadn't been trying to do the right thing by her, he would have been at home and the break-in might never have succeeded.

'And the dogs?'

He swerved to avoid a tree branch lying in the road. The movement swung her against him, the contact sending sensation surging through her. She clung to him for a moment until he brought the car into line and she could straighten up. The brief closeness was enough to set her heart pounding and for perspiration to veil her skin.

Yes, crazy to come with him.

'Glen thinks the dogs were thrown drugged meat,' Luke answered.

For a moment she felt disorientated, her original question almost driven from her mind. It was an effort to marshal her thoughts and make a sensible comment. 'Will they be all right?'

'I'll know when we get there.'

They drove the rest of the way in tense silence, punctuated only by the most necessary communication. She longed to reach out to him, to share his worry and lessen the burden of it if she could. But he didn't want her help. He didn't want anything to do with her. He must be as aware as she was that if not for her the break-in might not have happened at all.

Another black mark for her lifestyle, she thought unhappily, wondering if he was remembering that other time when too much publicity had cost him everything he'd held dear.

Against his better judgement, he'd supported her tonight—and look how it had turned out. He must regret getting involved with her in any capacity.

By the time they reached Hilltop, her nerves were so on edge that the slightest touch of Luke's hand on her arm made her jump.

'It's all right, we're here. I thought you were asleep,' he said into the sudden well of silence which fell after he switched off the engine.

She squared her shoulders. He had enough to worry about without adding her own concerns. 'I'm fine,' she insisted. She saw that the house was brightly lit

from end to end. Several strange cars were parked
outside.

'Probably the police,' Luke said, reading her
glance. 'Glen said he called them as soon as he discovered the break-in.' He leaned closer. 'You needn't
get involved. You're here now, but it might be easier
for you if you stayed in the background and let me
deal with everything. There's no need for both of us
to be put through this.'

She was already involved, in ways he couldn't begin to imagine. 'I didn't insist on coming to sit back
and watch. I want to help.'

He opened her door and helped her with the cum-
bersome gown. She wished there had been time for
her to change before setting off, or that she had left
some clothes at Hilltop. But she'd taken them all
home with her. There was nothing to be done except
accompany him into the house as she was.

After the darkened roads, the house lights were daz-
zling. Several police officers were checking surfaces
and points of entry while Glen was being interviewed
by a woman in plain clothes.

Seeing Luke, Glen came over and introduced the
senior officer on the case.

'Damn, I'm sorry about this,' Glen told Luke. 'If I
hadn't been distracted by that brush-fire...'

'The place could have burned down and I'd be
much worse off,' Luke pointed out. His sea-dark gaze
made a sweeping assessment of the scene. 'What was
taken?'

Glen's relief was palpable. 'Not much, it seems. It
could have been kids, judging by the senseless
vandalism.'

The detective consulted her notes. 'The thieves mainly concentrated on your office, Mr Ansfield. It's completely wrecked, as if they were looking for something they didn't find.'

Sarah drew a sharp breath. 'Your research material for the book!' The thieves must have read about Luke accompanying her to the awards presentation, and had taken advantage of the opportunity to raid his files.

The detective raised an eyebrow. 'You seem to know something about this, Miss…'

'Fox, Sarah Fox,' she supplied. 'I was working with Mr Ansfield on his biography.'

'Which wasn't the only book being written about me,' Luke added. 'My competitors made threats intended to stop me writing my own book before theirs came out.'

'And you didn't stop so they came here hoping to slow your work down enough so they could beat you to the punch?' the detective anticipated. 'Why didn't you report these threats?'

'There was no hard evidence. I didn't think things would go this far.' Even Luke sounded shaken at the lengths the other writers were evidently prepared to go to make sure their book came out first.

The detective looked dubious. 'Maybe next time you'll let us do our job before it comes to this. We'll need you to check everything, including manuscripts, computer files, whatever else you were working on, and give us a list of what's missing. Then I'll want a statement from both of you about these alleged threats. Fortunately your assistant got back to the house in time to get a glimpse of the thieves and part of the numberplate of their vehicle, so there's a good chance we can apprehend them quickly.'

When the detective read out the partial number-plate, it nagged at Sarah for some reason. Somewhere she'd seen a vehicle with a similar plate, but her tired mind refused to yield the details. Maybe it would come to her later.

She followed Luke into the study where they had worked together so recently. Recalling the satisfying work, even the fierce arguments, she felt a pang. She had never thought it would turn out like this.

If Luke *had* been here during the break-in, instead of with her, the consequence might have been disastrous.

He saw her turn pale and slid a hand under her elbow. 'It's okay. The papers can be replaced. No one was hurt.'

She forced a smile and knew it didn't quite reach her eyes. 'I know, but I can't help thinking—if you'd been here...'

'But I wasn't. And, thank God, neither was Glen.' He lowered his mouth so he spoke for her ears alone. 'Now our competition have stuck their greedy necks out, they may just get them chopped off for their trouble.'

'But the book...all your hard work...'

'I have back ups of all the disks, safely filed away. I doubt they found those,' he said tautly. 'If that's what they were even looking for.'

'Oh, Luke, I'm so thankful you came to the banquet tonight.' She didn't care if he misunderstood and thought it was for her own sake. The thought of him being hurt in any way was more than she could bear.

But he didn't misunderstand. 'That makes two of us.'

The warmth of his smile flowed into her, giving her the strength to start sorting through the chaos to help identify whether anything was missing. Everything was in such disarray it would take ages to sort things out, and she said so to the uniformed policeman who joined them in the study.

He regarded her with interest. 'Aren't you Sarah Fox?'

She nodded. 'Until recently I was working here on a book with Mr Ansfield.'

The officer grinned. 'You were on TV tonight. I saw most of the show before I came on duty.'

She plucked at the folds of her gown. 'We were both at the banquet after the show when Luke heard about…this.'

Instead of taking her hint to stick to the subject at hand, the officer proffered a notebook. 'Can I have your autograph for my daughter?'

She felt Luke's eyes boring into her as she reluctantly accepted the notepad and scrawled her name. Surely he couldn't think she welcomed the attention at a time like this? She handed the pad back. 'I'd better make a start on this mess.'

'Your dress is sensational,' the officer persisted. 'Were you nervous, appearing on a big show like that? You looked as cool as a cucumber.'

Before she could reply, the senior detective attracted the officer's attention in the other room. He grinned at her as he left. 'Wait till I tell my daughter I met you. She'll be thrilled.'

Luke wasn't at all thrilled, she saw from his closed

expression. 'When you've finished, could you check these files? Quite a few seem to be missing,' he said in a cool, detached voice. The warmth of a moment ago had evaporated.

She went over to his desk. 'It isn't my fault he refused to be sidetracked,' she pointed out, hurt by his apparent withdrawal. 'I tried to keep his mind on the job.'

'No need to apologise. I understand,' he assured her. 'You're probably the first celebrity he's met.'

His tolerance was somehow harder to take than his censure, because it underlined his conviction that they belonged in different worlds. The officer's reaction only emphasised the point.

Luckily there were no more such incidents and the rest of the investigation took little time. Glen had disturbed the thieves before they vandalised more than the office. If he hadn't dealt with the brush-fire speedily, and headed straight back to the house, the outcome might have been different.

It was almost dawn by the time the police left. Glen had taken the dogs to the local veterinarian, who had assured him the sedative was mild and they would recover with no ill effects.

Sarah wished she could say the same for herself. She couldn't remember when she had felt this exhausted.

'You'd better spend the night here,' Luke said when they were alone at last. From the lack of inflection in his voice, he might have been offering her coffee.

He sounded so tired that she hadn't the heart to insist on being driven home, although spending a night under his roof was the last thing she wanted to do.

'I don't have any clothes with me,' she said diffidently. Her gown looked decidedly wilted. She could hardly spend the night wearing it.

'I'll lend you a T-shirt and a bathrobe for now, and something to wear home in the morning.' He passed a hand across his eyes. 'You shouldn't have insisted on coming with me.'

Because he didn't want her here? 'I was glad to help,' she declared. If it meant she spent a sleepless night imagining him in bed only a few feet away, it was the price she would have to pay.

For want of a distraction, she began listlessly to tidy up the mess left by the investigators. Luke lifted files from her hands. 'It will keep until morning. You look all-in.'

'I am tired. But I must shower first or I'll never get to sleep.'

He nodded, his face shuttered and unreadable. 'Go ahead. You can use the same room as before. The bed's made up and there are towels in the *en suite* bathroom. Help yourself to anything you need.'

The one thing she needed wasn't hers for the asking, but she compressed her lips on the betraying observation. If Luke could keep this encounter neutral, then so could she—if it killed her. 'Thank you,' she said, striving to match his air of cool detachment.

'I'll bring the robe and T-shirt in and leave them on the bed while you're in the shower.'

She nodded her thanks and turned away.

Without her things, the room looked as remote as a hotel suite, which was probably just as well. Making herself at home at Hilltop wasn't part of her plans. Knowing how she felt about Luke made staying under his roof the most exquisite form of torture.

The shower was blissful. The massaging effect of the powerful jets did much to restore her sense of wellbeing. She stayed under the refreshing spray for as long as possible, giving Luke the chance to leave the clothes for her and retire to his own room before she emerged.

Swathing herself in one of the generously sized towels she found in the bathroom, she padded barefoot through to the bedroom then stopped dead in her tracks. Luke was just placing the garments on the bed.

He had showered too and wore only a light robe, open to the waist, and no shoes. She pulled in a steadying breath and inhaled the leathery scent of aftershave lotion.

His reaction was carefully neutral. 'Feeling better now?'

Two could play this game. 'Yes, thank you.'

Then she glanced down and saw his hands, clenched tightly against his sides. His rigidly controlled expression was supposed to remind her of her place, which was as far away from here as possible, but once again his body language gave her a different message. He was not as impervious to her as he wanted her to think.

A need so savage it was like a hunger ripped through her, almost tearing away her veneer of insouciance. A tremor shook her and she clutched the towel more tightly around herself, as if its thin protection could arm her against the torrent of feelings he provoked in her.

She made herself look towards the bed, although her neck felt rigid. 'Are those for me?'

He picked up a robe which was made of some velvety fabric in a rich amber colour. 'A gift from my mother. I've never worn it,' he explained, although she hadn't asked.

It looked like the sort of garment a woman would choose for a man she—loved. She tensed as he held it out to her.

'Better put it on, you're trembling. Must be cold or delayed reaction, or both.'

She was trembling, but it wasn't from cold. The tremors had another source entirely. She almost smiled as he turned his head away and closed his eyes. 'I won't look while you slip into this.'

She tried to sound devil-may-care when it was the last thing she felt. 'After changing in a studio filled with technicians, modesty should be the least of my worries.'

Contrarily, she found she wanted him to see her as she shed the towel, wanted him to appreciate her—to realise what he was giving up? Surely she couldn't be that petty?

A muscle worked at his throat but he kept his face averted as she turned around and slid her arms into the robe he held for her. The material felt sensuously soft against her damp skin. The silky folds fell around her, almost swamping her.

When she'd pulled the robe around her, he opened his eyes and drew a deep breath. 'It could never look like that on me.'

Beyond the ache in her throat she found a sufficiently light answer. 'At least on you it would *fit*.'

Something indefinable flickered in the gaze with which he held her. With deliberate care he began to turn up the sleeves of the robe, the gesture emphasising her small size against his. It was an oddly parental act, but the resulting turmoil inside her was anything but child-like. She had never felt so conscious of her femininity as she did at that moment.

He finished with one sleeve and began on the other, his breathing growing more and more laboured. She could hardly breathe for the tension coiling through her. 'I think that's enough,' she said huskily. Much more and she would forget entirely all the reasons why they should not get involved.

One look at Luke's intense expression told her it might be too late already. Probably was. Was.

Too late for what? As he slid his hands inside the ample folds of the soft robe she thought there was something vital she ought to remember, but all she could think of was how good it felt to have him hold her at long last.

When he crushed her against him the velvet slid across her skin, heightening sensation until every one of a thousand nerve-endings awakened to tingling life. It was as if he was caressing every part of her, so sensitised was she to his slightest touch.

How she had yearned for this, she recognised as his mouth travelled across her forehead and traced a line down her nose, seeking her lips with slow but unerring precision.

She struggled to shape a refusal, before this got completely out of hand, but what came out was, 'Kiss me, Luke.'

A teasing playfulness sprang into his eyes. 'Ask me nicely.'

How could she even think straight when she wanted him with every fibre of her being? 'Please kiss me,' she appealed hoarsely.

It was the last thing she should have said, and astonishment rippled through her as she heard her betraying plea. She *did* want him to kiss her, wanted him to do much more if she was honest, but that didn't make it right.

Then he began a slow, sensuous exploration of her body beneath the robe, and she was lost. Closing her eyes, she tilted her face upwards, unconsciously parting her lips to emphasise the invitation she shouldn't have issued but couldn't take back if her life depended on it.

When he kissed her it was like a homecoming. As she slid her hands up to link around his neck the sleeves of the robe fell to her elbows, and the weight tugged the robe open to the waist, but she was too preoccupied with tasting all she could of him to notice or care.

'Sarah.' His husky use of her name was like a thousand volts of electricity coursing through her. As his mouth fastened over hers she felt his fingers brush the straining mounds of her breasts. His lips were like fire, searing her to the core.

With a tug, he released the cord holding the robe and it fell open completely. He stepped inside the circle of fabric and held her close to him, making her vividly aware that there was only one place this could end.

Through the haze of joy and pleasure surging

within her, a tiny alarm bell shrilled. If they made love, it would be all the harder to leave in the morning and return to her own life.

She had no doubt Luke would still insist on sending her away. For him it meant an interlude of pleasure, no strings attached. For her the strings would stretch and stretch from him, all the way back to her real life, entangling her in needs and dreams which had no hope of fulfilment.

He sensed her hesitation. 'What is it, Sarah? A change of heart?'

'No,' she whispered. Her heart was the one thing which *hadn't* changed. Knowing what might have happened to him tonight only emphasised the depths of her feelings for him.

He let her hair drift through his fingers, sending a spill of desire all along her spine. 'I know you want me.'

'Yes.' There was no point in denying it. She'd been telling him so with every breath.

'And you must know how much I want you.'

'Yes.' No point denying that, either.

His look gentled and he scooped her into his arms, carrying her to the bed where he deposited her as if she were infinitely precious. 'Then nothing can be wrong. I'll protect you, I promise, if that's your concern.' Assuming the question was settled, he leaned over to kiss her more deeply, covering her heated body with his own.

The contact sent white fire along her veins, and she found herself returning his kisses with a passion which finally gave release to the desire pent up inside her for so long.

She loved him. Nothing else mattered. Not tomorrow. Not the heartache she was storing up for herself. Nothing except a need so elemental it drove every coherent thought out of her head.

The minutes when he stood up to peel off his own robe and make good his promise to protect her felt like hours. After the heat of his touch she felt chilled by his absence, seconds long though it was. Dear heaven, if the briefest loss could feel like this, how could she endure a lifetime without him?

She drove the fear away by opening her arms to him as he lowered himself gently over her. For a long time he simply kissed every inch of her, until the urgency of wanting him became too powerful to resist.

His own need blazed at her from eyes dark with passion, but he held himself back, muscles taut with his restraint, offering her the gift of his patience, loving her so totally that she wanted to weep.

All the while he murmured tenderly to her, the actual words lost in the softness of his voice against her throat, her cheeks, her forehead, her mouth. She thought she answered in kind, but the words didn't seem to matter. She could barely think straight for the maelstrom building and building and building within her.

'Luke, love me, please.'

And he did, banking fires of desire inside her with every exquisite surge of sensation, until she ached with wanting him.

The emotional depths to which he plunged her equalled only the heights of joy beyond. Thus far her life had had nothing with which to compare the experience, so she didn't even try. Some things were to be lived, not analysed. She lived them with him, loving him for all the tomorrows that could never be.

Afterwards she nestled into the curve of his arm, his fingers resting lightly on the softness of her breast, her breathing gradually quieting as she pondered the recklessness of what she had invited.

Next morning she awoke to find herself alone in the bed. Bleakness swept over her. She should have expected this. She had made love with Luke knowing full well that it would change nothing between them. It should come as no surprise to find she was right.

Before slipping away, he had pulled the covers over her without waking her. He had also left the T-shirt and a pair of jeans on a chair beside the bed. His message was all too clear. Last night had been wonderful, but today they were back in the real world.

She got up and dressed slowly, the faintly dragging sensation in her muscles a poignant reminder of paradise found—and lost.

The jeans swam on her, a further reminder of last night. She used the belt from the robe to hold them in place and allowed the loose T-shirt to hang over them. The effect was a bit Little Orphan Annie, but it would do until she got home. She could imagine her neighbours' faces if Luke brought her home in the middle of the morning and she was still wearing the gown from the night before.

Glen was in the kitchen preparing breakfast when she arrived. 'Just coffee for me, thanks,' she said, looking around.

'Luke's gone to see the police,' Glen explained, intercepting the look. 'He told me to let you sleep.'

Alarm clutched at her. 'What's happened?'

'The detectives traced the car from the break-in. It belongs to Richard Nero. Luke has to identify some of his computer disks and files found in the vehicle.'

'Richard was in league with the writers of the other book?' Her voice reflected her shock. She'd known Richard hated her, but she could hardly believe he would go this far.

Heartsick, she sat down. No wonder the partial numberplate had struck her as familiar. It belonged to an off-road vehicle Richard had occasionally driven to the studio.

She knew him well enough to understand how his mind worked. His show was failing, the ratings in steady decline. Working with the other writers must have seemed like a heaven-sent opportunity to snare an exclusive story and get back at Sarah all at the same time. It was just the sort of adventure which would appeal to Richard's devious mind, and he wouldn't stop to think of the consequences, or see that what he was doing was actually criminal.

That his strategy hadn't worked was little consolation. It was her fault that Richard had become interested in Luke's activities in the first place. It was also likely that the promise of publicity on Richard's show had increased the determination of the other writers to get into print first, driving them to break in to Luke's office. Without Richard's involvement, they might not have gone so far. How could she face Luke after this?

She pushed aside the coffee. 'I'd like to go home as soon as you're ready to drive me, Glen.'

'Wouldn't you rather wait for Luke?'

How could she when all she had done was complicate his life? She shook her head. 'Tell him I said goodbye, and tell him—tell him he was right after all.'

Glen looked worried, sensing her distress. 'What are you going to do?'

She gave a brittle laugh. 'Talk to my agent, sign a new contract.' And try to go on in spite of a heart already shattering into little pieces at the prospect.

CHAPTER ELEVEN

'CHEER up. This is more like a wake than a celebration.'

Kitty was right. Sarah's long face didn't belong at the lunch they had arranged to celebrate the signing of her new contract. It should have been a dream come true, but all it did was emphasise the emptiness in her life since she'd returned to her apartment alone.

If only she and Luke hadn't made love she might have found the loneliness bearable, but every night was a fresh reminder of what might have been.

Not that she doubted the rightness of her decision. After the headlines resulting from Richard Nero's arrest, Luke had apparently left town altogether, to avoid the fanfare, according to Kitty, who had coyly mentioned going to Hilltop to see Glen.

'I wanted his recipe for blueberry muffins,' was the only explanation Sarah could prise out of her. Once Kitty had confirmed that Luke was out of town, nothing else seemed to matter.

He hadn't come after her, probably agreeing with the message she had asked Glen to pass on. She had tried to make it true by getting on with her life. Today's lunch proved how well she was succeeding.

Now all she had to do was banish Luke from her thoughts and enjoy the fruits of her success. Ironically, she was doing exactly what he'd wanted her to do.

Some sixth sense warned her even before Kitty's face lit up in recognition. 'Luke, how good to see you.'

Thanking her stars for the few seconds she needed to drop her mask of indifference into place, Sarah turned slowly. 'Hello, Luke. I didn't know you were in town.'

'I got back this morning and needed a few things before driving to Hilltop,' he explained. He sounded as cool and distant as any casual acquaintance. Only the blazing look in his eyes gave any hint that there was any more between them.

'Join us for lunch,' Kitty urged, impervious to Sarah's startled reaction. 'We're celebrating Sarah's new contract.'

Some of the fire died in his eyes but his mouth curved into a smile. 'I can't stay, but congratulations, Sarah. Your show is bound to be a huge success.'

Then he was gone, melting into the crowd of shoppers with long-legged strides which ate at her spirits as they ate up the distance between them.

Every instinct she possessed urged her to call him back, do anything but let him walk away for ever. But she did nothing. She had made the bargain with herself. Now she had to stick to it.

She hadn't expected it to be easy. But neither had she thought it would tear at her very soul.

Kitty gave her a puzzled look. 'What was that about your *show* being a success?'

'He probably thinks I'm going back to television,' Sarah supplied.

Her friend's eyebrows lifted. 'You mean he doesn't know about your *book* contract?'

Sarah's shoulders dropped. 'Whether I anchor *Coast to Coast* or write a bestselling novel, it's still a public activity. Look at the problems he had because of me last time.'

'So you walked away rather than drag him into the spotlight with you? Are you nuts?'

Startled, Sarah looked at her friend. 'What?'

'That man is the best thing that's happened to you since I've known you. You can't let this come between you.'

'It already has,' Sarah said flatly. She hadn't told Kitty about the reason behind Luke's hatred of publicity but she did so now. She could trust Kitty to keep the confidence to herself.

The other woman whistled softly. 'I agree it's a big stumbling block, but look at the drama over Luke's own book. He fielded it successfully without caving in. Thanks to your friend, Richard Nero, there won't be a competing book, so it's up to Luke whether he goes ahead with his or not.'

Sarah grimaced at Kitty's description of Richard as her friend. He and two writers had been charged with the break-in at Hilltop. It had ended any chance of the unauthorised biography being published, or of Richard working in television again.

'Luke's tough. He can handle himself,' Kitty insisted.

'I know, but he shouldn't have to on my account.'

Kitty leaned forward, toying with her Caesar salad. 'Was he the reason you turned down *Coast to Coast*?'

'No. He helped me to see I could do other things besides television journalism, but the decision was my own.'

'And you do them well,' Kitty endorsed. 'Who'd have believed you could score a contract with a major publisher on the strength of a twelve-page book outline and a few sample chapters?'

Sarah laughed. 'My agent certainly didn't. Phil was horrified when I told him what I wanted to do. But he changed his mind when the contract came through.'

'Which brings us back to our celebration.' Kitty lifted her wine-glass. 'To you and your success.'

It galled Sarah to drink to success when it was the very thing driving her and Luke apart, but she lifted her own glass.

'To our friendship,' she countered. It was the one constant in her life lately, enabling her to carry on despite the gnawing ache inside her. Time healed all wounds, she told herself. Just how much time would be required for this particular wound, she didn't like to contemplate.

A glance at her watch brought her scrambling to her feet. 'I have to go. I'm meeting a writer from the *Gold Coast Herald* to talk about the new book contract,' she explained.

Kitty grinned. 'Make sure you mention that your best friend has the largest photo library on the coast. I can use the publicity, even if you can't.'

Sarah smiled back. 'I'll do my best.'

She did better than that. During the course of the interview about her career change she managed to convince the journalist to interview Kitty for a separate feature story. It was small enough reward for all Kitty's support over the years.

Two days later Kitty rang back to thank her, then

mentioned, almost as an afterthought, 'I'm driving to Hilltop this afternoon to see Glen. He wants my advice on choosing a camera. I'd love the company if you want to come.'

Sarah's throat closed and a swaying sensation made her clutch the edge of the telephone table. 'I don't think so, Kitty. I have to work on my book.'

There was a short silence. 'Luke won't be there,' Kitty said quietly. 'Glen tells me he's in Brisbane on business.'

Even so, the idea of returning to Hilltop was more than Sarah could bear. Luke would be there even when he wasn't. His presence already pervaded her life. How was she to forget about him if she kept looking back?

Still, it was as tempting an invitation as she would ever receive. Hilltop was where Luke had kissed her in the cavern under the fig tree. In the house was the room where they had made such spectacular love.

'No,' she said, unaware of having spoken aloud. She would not turn his house into some sort of shrine to a lost love. She had made her choice. Life would go on. It had to.

'Okay, I get the message,' Kitty said, sounding startled.

'Sorry, I didn't mean to snap. I guess I'm still a little sensitive on the subject of Luke.'

Kitty laughed. 'Try a *lot* sensitive. Are you sure you're all right, Sarah? Is there anything I can do?'

Sarah injected warmth into her voice. 'I'm perfectly fine and there's nothing you can do—except go see Glen and talk photography. I didn't know he was an enthusiast.'

'Let's say he's working on it,' Kitty said mysteriously. They chatted a little longer about inconsequential things, then hung up, leaving Sarah to wonder about Kitty and Glen.

While she'd been at Hilltop Glen had remained in the background. Although any man would pale into the background beside Luke, she accepted. Glen was pleasant and capable, even if no Luke Ansfield. Did Kitty see something in the man that Sarah had missed?

She dismissed the speculation from her mind. She was no expert on her own love life, so it was foolhardy to involve herself in Kitty's affairs. She decided to make good her plan to work on the new book.

Her agent had sold the book on the strength of the outline and three sample chapters, maybe ten thousand words in all. Some ninety thousand words remained to be written, so the sooner she got on with it the better.

Trusting the maxim that said, 'write what you know', she had developed a story about three sisters who started from nothing and succeeded brilliantly in widely differing professions.

Her book would explore the relationship between them, and the idea of sisterhood in general.

There was a risk that readers would confuse her fictional sisters with Sarah's own family but it wasn't about them, although their experiences would help her story to ring true.

Snapping on the answering machine so she could work undisturbed, she turned on her computer and started writing.

It had grown too dark to see the screen properly by

the time she stretched her cramped muscles and sat back. The pages pouring from the printer were testimony to her hours of productivity. She felt exhausted and slightly punch-drunk from living so intensely in her fictional world, but she was exhilarated too. The book was on its way.

Heading towards the kitchen, intending to make coffee to revive herself, she turned on the lights to find a telltale blinking on her answering machine.

She rewound the tape. The caller was Kitty. 'Hi, Sarah. Guess you're in the throes so I won't disturb you. But Glen tells me Luke's appearing on the *Tony Lawrence Show* tonight. I know you don't want to see him ever again, so I thought I'd warn you against turning the show on and catching him. Don't say I never do anything for you. Bye.'

Suddenly Sarah's chest felt tight. She made herself take deep, calming breaths. Oh, Kitty was clever. By warning Sarah against putting the *Tony Lawrence Show* on she had made it almost irresistible.

'Serve you right if I don't watch it,' she snapped at the innocent-looking machine. She imagined Kitty's howls of protest. 'But I was only taking your advice,' she answered the imaginary response.

She fought a tug-of-war with herself. First she thought she wouldn't look at the show. Why put herself through such torment? She would make her hot drink and go to bed with a good book.

The mantel clock chimed the hour. The show was already starting. By the time she made coffee and got ready for bed it would be half-over. The decision would be made.

No decision was still a decision, she reminded herself. Damn you, Kitty. If you hadn't left the message I'd have gone to bed and been none the wiser.

Despite the pep-talk, she found herself walking to the television and switching it on, her movements jerky as she battled with herself.

The theme music ended and the band-leader introduced the star, Tony Lawrence. In spite of her wound-tight nerves, Sarah smiled. She'd met Tony several times at television industry functions and liked him enormously. From the capable, charismatic way he presented his show, no one would guess the war of nerves he fought with himself before each programme.

He looked coolly attractive as he ran through an amusing opening monologue about his experiences with a car repairer. 'And speaking of cars,' he went on, making Sarah tense, 'after the break my guest is the world's fastest man on wheels. Five times Grand Prix world champion, Luke Ansfield, speaking out for the first time in four years.'

Forget the coffee. With shaking hands she poured herself a glass of brandy. She almost never drank alone, but this time she didn't hesitate. Why she would need a dose of Dutch courage just to watch Luke on television was something she needed to examine.

Kitty had said she was overly sensitive where Luke was concerned, and, as usual, her friend was right. But she couldn't go through life turning into a quivering wreck every time Luke's name was mentioned.

Making herself watch him would be good therapy, she rationalised. Seeing enough of him might desensitise her to his attraction.

She would have to do a lot better than this, she told herself, wrapping shaking fingers around the brandy glass. The drink was untouched, her fevered brain needing no additional stimulation beyond the sight of Luke striding purposefully onto the set.

For someone who hated publicity as much as he did, he looked remarkably self-assured. He wore an open-necked Lacoste shirt, the colour of red wine, over tailored cream trousers.

Her trained eye searched for TV make-up, but the healthy glow of his skin was entirely natural, the diamond-bright sparkle in his eyes the product of an inner fire she recognised. He radiated confidence and—something more—a hard core of purpose. To achieve what?

She fumed with impatience while Tony Lawrence introduced his guest. Many fans from Luke's racing days were in the studio audience, judging by the wild applause. She waited hungrily for each glimpse the camera allowed her of him.

The inevitable film footage of his racing triumphs followed, and Sarah's heart leapt into her mouth at the sight of him flirting with danger around every curve in the track. Even though she knew he was safe, watching the man she loved dice with death was an agonising experience.

Thank heaven he didn't race any more, she thought after watching a scene where only his hair-trigger reflexes had saved him from disaster. Women loved these men. How could they endure it?

The interview set returned, and she released the breath she was unaware of holding. Seeing Luke well and whole, sitting so easily in a chair opposite Tony Lawrence, was like a gift.

The talk show host's next words galvanised her afresh. 'Luke has promised us an exclusive preview of his autobiography—a book which almost didn't get written, did it, Luke?'

Luke nodded. 'I originally started writing it to head off an unauthorised version. After the writers of that book were arrested, breaking into my home, I toyed with abandoning the project, then decided to go ahead, to close the door on that part of my life.'

Tony Lawrence leaned closer. 'I understand you talk for the first time about a tragedy you've kept secret until now?'

A shadow darkened Luke's ruggedly handsome features. 'Hardly secret, but not widely reported in Australia.'

Sarah sat forward as a photo of a vivacious dark-haired woman was shown. The host's voice-over described her as Luke's one-time fiancée, killed in a botched kidnapping attempt soon after he'd won his fifth world championship.

'At the time, the media accused me of contributing to her death by recklessly chasing the kidnapper's car,' Luke said as the camera returned to him. 'I even believed it myself for a time, and I started dodging the limelight when I couldn't stand to read about myself any longer.' He took a deep breath. 'While researching for the book I uncovered evidence that my fiancée had helped her so-called kidnapper to stage the abduction to extort money from me.'

'And the high-speed chase in which she died?'

'Her own doing. Once she knew I'd seen them, she

couldn't allow me to catch up or I'd have recognised the ''kidnapper'' as a friend I'd seen her with earlier.'

'She was pregnant at the time, wasn't she?' Tony Lawrence prompted gently.

Luke massaged his jaw with one hand. 'For years I thought the child was mine. But her accomplice was identified as the real father. He was a criminal, with friends in high places who had the evidence suppressed. If I hadn't started digging through old records for my book, I'd never have found out the truth.'

The book had proved his salvation, Sarah thought, blinking hard. Luke wasn't to blame for the death of the woman and her baby. Her own deceit was the real cause. Sarah wanted to cheer.

Tony Lawrence gave a grave nod. 'What made you decide to tell the story publicly now?'

Luke smiled faintly, the lines around his eyes deepening in the glare of the studio lights. With all her heart, Sarah wished she were there.

She didn't know why he'd chosen to share his personal tragedy with the world now—unless it was to send a message to her. Didn't he know she would rather die than put him through this? Nothing was worth such a sacrifice.

But Luke had his own ideas. 'Call it excess emotional baggage,' he told Tony Lawrence. 'As well as explaining a past tragedy, writing the book helped me sort out my priorities.'

'And what *are* those priorities?'

Luke's face softened. 'A beautiful lady named Sarah. I've made some monumental mistakes in my life, but letting her go would be the biggest. That's why I asked if I could use your show to propose to her here and now.'

The brandy glass slid from her nerveless fingers onto the carpet. Was she dreaming? Could Luke really mean what he was saying?

Tony Lawrence grinned. 'For a man who's notoriously publicity-shy, this is a big step, isn't it?'

Luke nodded. 'Television is her world. I want to do this her way, so she's in no doubt about how I feel.'

The camera moved in closer and the screen filled with Luke's image as he looked, it seemed, directly at her. 'I love you, Sarah. I want to marry you.'

Sarah felt the tears sliding down her cheeks. She had a lot of company. A shot of the studio audience showed many of them dabbing their eyes.

They couldn't feel half as stunned as she did at this moment. She barely heard Tony Lawrence say, 'There you are—a marriage proposal from the King of Formula One racing to his queen. We'll be back after this break.'

Luke loved her and wanted to marry her. Could it possibly be true? How did one answer such a proposal?

She knew what she wanted to say, but Luke was a hundred kilometres away in a Brisbane television studio. She ached for him with a longing which was like a physical pain.

Her mind reeled. Being compelled to write the book had led Luke to uncover the truth about his fiancée's death. Now he was forced to accept that not all media exposure ended in tragedy. Sometimes it even helped to heal. The biggest obstacle between him and Sarah was an obstacle no longer.

By proposing on television Luke had shown his willingness to share her world. No matter that he wouldn't have to. The offer was more than enough.

She had to do something: pack a bag, drive to Brisbane, go to him, be with him, love him.

Before she could do any of them, the doorbell rang and she frowned with impatience. She didn't need a caller now, when she should be on her way to Luke's side.

Steeling herself to get rid of whoever it was as fast as possible, she almost collapsed when she found Luke himself leaning against the doorframe. His love-filled eyes met her startled gaze. 'Hello, Sarah. May I come in?'

'But what are you…? How did you…?' Where was the unflappable journalist now? Her brain felt like cotton wool and her legs threatened to give way under her.

'Shouldn't you invite me in? Or would you prefer our entire relationship to be conducted in the public eye?'

His humour broke through her shock. He followed her inside and gathered her into his arms. 'I've dreamed of this moment all day. I love you so much.'

'I know. I heard.' She was so shaky she could barely speak, knew only that she was finally where she wanted and needed to be—safe in Luke's embrace. 'You must have taped the *Tony Lawrence* segment,' she said, her voice husky with love for him. She could hardly believe he was here.

He nodded, threading his fingers through her hair

as he rained kisses over her upturned face. 'I didn't break any speed limits driving back here, but I was sorely tempted.'

She turned dazed eyes to him, picturing him racing to her side. It was all too confusing. First the proposal, now this. 'You said what we had was a fantasy. Am I still dreaming? Or did you really propose marriage to me on national television?'

He flicked gentle kisses onto each eyelid in turn, then rested her face against his shoulder and stroked her hair. 'It's no fantasy, Sarah. I only told you it was so you would feel free to follow your dream. But I found I couldn't live without you.' A pulse beat wildly at his throat. 'Which bothers you the most— me proposing or being asked on national television?'

Nestled against the curve of his shoulder, she drew a shuddering breath. 'Both seem a bit overwhelming at the moment.'

She felt him nod before he gently lifted her head to meet his eyes. 'I wanted to show you that I love you as you are, even if it means sharing you with your public for the rest of our lives. I'll be wildly jealous but I can handle it.'

A thrill rocketed through her. 'I never doubted you could. It was me who wanted to change.'

He frowned. 'You? Then why did you sign a new contract to host *Coast to Coast*?'

He still didn't know, she realised as a frisson of pleasure surged along her spine. He had accepted her as he believed she was, being prepared to change his whole way of life to accommodate what he thought she wanted. Could any woman possibly feel more loved?

She gave a gentle shake of her head. 'Kitty and I *were* celebrating a new contract, but it isn't for a television show.'

'Then what?'

She answered his questioning look with a small smile. 'You obviously didn't read yesterday's newspaper. The contract is with a publisher, for my first novel. After working on your book I got the writing bug.' She indicated the computer printouts festooning the couch, where she'd been editing them. 'See— Chapter One, first draft.'

His eyes gleamed. 'Here was I, all set to deal with your fame, only to find I'm going to have a struggling writer on my hands.' He didn't sound in the least disappointed.

He drew her onto the couch and the manuscript pages fluttered unheeded to the floor. 'I'm still waiting for your answer.'

Tears of pure happiness gathered in her eyes. 'You've had my answer for a long time. I just didn't know it. Yes, I'll marry you. I love you so much it hurts.'

He kissed her so fiercely that a tight band constricted around her heart. 'Then I'll have to kiss the hurt better, won't I?'

The thought of how he might go about it set her senses on fire. 'Please,' she urged.

He obliged so thoroughly that she was dizzy from anoxia by the time he allowed her to come up for air. Somehow her clothes ended up on the floor alongside his, and the kissing better took a long, long time.

Afterwards, as she lay dreamily in the curve of his arm, she became distantly aware that the *Tony*

Lawrence Show was coming to a close. She'd forgotten the television was still on as she lost herself in the wonder of Luke's lovemaking. Now she started as she heard her name mentioned again. 'What did he say?'

'He was telling the audience that you said yes,' Luke supplied, his tone teasing.

She struggled around to look at him, supporting herself on one elbow. 'How could he know my answer if the show was taped earlier in the day?'

Luke kissed her with fiery possessiveness. 'Did you think I'd let you get away with any other answer? After I saw you with Kitty the other day, I knew I couldn't go one more day without you. Walking away was the hardest thing I've ever done, but I needed to think of exactly the right way to tell you how I felt.'

Only hours before she'd believed it was all over. Now his tone made it plain they were only beginning. Still, she couldn't let him have it all his own way. 'What if I had said no?' she asked, a smile softening the question.

He sobered, but his eyes danced. 'Then I'd have had to make love to you until you changed your mind.'

Warmth flooded through her as she made a face. 'I may have been a little hasty. You can't rush these decisions, you know.'

He gave a throaty growl. 'In that case, I know how to convince you.'

She almost purred. It was exactly what she wanted him to do, and she didn't mind if it took the rest of their lives together.

EPILOGUE

'HAPPY birthday to you, happy birthday to you, happy birthday dear Jason, happy birthday to you.'

The dark-haired little boy looked bemused but impressed by all the attention as Sarah helped him to blow out the two fat candles on the cake, which was shaped like a castle at her son's request.

She was dying to see his face when he saw the almost-life-sized castle Luke had bought for his birthday. It was a combination of climbing centre, sandpit and toy fort all in one.

They had agreed to save the surprise until the rest of the family arrived, later in the day. This small celebration was for Jason's benefit and the other two-year-olds from his playgroup.

Thinking of her parents, who would join them soon, Sarah smiled. She had never dreamed, when she married Luke, that she would become the apple of their eye. Obviously having one daughter in the Senate and another with her own fashion label couldn't compare with the appeal of their first grandson. Even her own modest success with her first novel, while pleasing her parents, hadn't reduced them to tears of joy as Jason's birth had done.

'Look at Daddy as Mummy cuts the cake,' Luke urged.

Sarah glanced up to see Luke aiming his video camera at her. Since the birth of their son it had become his favourite toy. Quite a switch for someone who had avoided publicity like the plague when she'd met him. Now he wanted to document every moment of Jason's existence.

She grimaced. 'Film Jason, but not me. I look terrible.'

He grinned. 'You weren't always so camera-shy.'

'I wasn't six months pregnant then,' she reminded him.

Kitty moved closer. 'I hope you won't be too busy with your next production to spare time to attend my wedding.'

Sarah shook her head. 'For you and Glen, we'll make time. It's wonderful that you two got together.'

'How could I go past a guy who makes such great blueberry muffins?' Kitty asked. 'And with a surname like Zammit, it was meant to be.'

Funny, it had never occurred to Sarah to ask Glen his surname. But she had to admit it had saved Kitty working her way through the entire alphabet. Her friend had never looked happier.

Fending off the excited Dobermanns romping around their feet, Kitty began to hand out slices of birthday cake. Luke took the knife from Sarah and set it aside.

'Come here, woman. What makes you think you could look anything but beautiful to me?'

She looked down at her swelling figure. After almost three years, it amazed her to find the flame of their love burning more brightly than ever. Tears prickled her eyes, and she cursed the emotions which were so near the surface these days.

Luke heard the muffled sob and brushed the wetness away with a finger. 'Tears, darling?'

'Only of happiness,' she assured him. 'I can't wait for my parents and your mother and father to get here to make the party complete.'

Since Luke's book had been published, he and his adoptive parents had become reconciled. They had probably never expected him to write so generously about them in his autobiography. The book's success meant they were minor celebrities in their own right now, and Sarah suspected they loved every minute of it.

She was thrilled for Luke, and especially pleased for their children. With one set of grandparents on the land, a grandfather lecturing at university and a grandmother who doted unashamedly on them, their children had the best of all possible worlds.

And so, thought Sarah as she melted into her husband's loving embrace, did she.

MILLS & BOON®

Next Month's Romances

♡

Each month you can choose from a wide variety of romance novels from Mills & Boon. Below are the new titles to look out for next month from the Presents™ and Enchanted™ series.

Presents™

A NANNY FOR CHRISTMAS	Sara Craven
A FORBIDDEN DESIRE	Robyn Donald
THE WINTER BRIDE	Lynne Graham
THE PERFECT MATCH?	Penny Jordan
RED-HOT AND RECKLESS	Miranda Lee
BARGAIN WITH THE WIND	Kathleen O'Brien
THE DISOBEDIENT BRIDE	Elizabeth Power
ALL MALE	Kay Thorpe

Enchanted™

SANTA'S SPECIAL DELIVERY	Val Daniels
THE MARRIAGE PACT	Elizabeth Duke
A MIRACLE FOR CHRISTMAS	Grace Green
ACCIDENTAL WIFE	Day Leclaire
ONE NIGHT BEFORE CHRISTMAS	Catherine Leigh
A SINGULAR HONEYMOON	Leigh Michaels
A HUSBAND FOR CHRISTMAS	Emma Richmond
TEMPORARY GIRLFRIEND	Jessica Steele

Available from WH Smith, John Menzies, Volume One, Forbuoys, Martins, Tesco, Asda, Safeway and other paperback stockists.

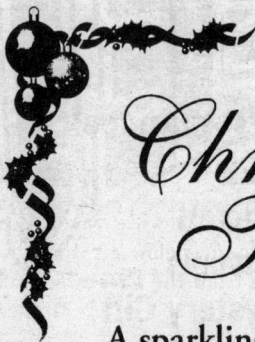

MILLS & BOON®

Christmas Treats

**A sparkling new anthology
—the perfect Christmas gift!**

Celebrate the season with a taste of love in this
delightful collection of brand-new short stories
combining the pleasures of food and love.

Figgy Pudding
by PENNY JORDAN
All the Trimmings
by LINDSAY ARMSTRONG
A Man For All Seasonings
by DAY LECLAIRE

And, as an extra treat, we've included the
authors' own recipe ideas in this
collection—because no yuletide would be
complete without...Christmas Dinner!

FREE!

FOUR FREE
specially selected
Enchanted™ novels
<u>PLUS</u> a FREE Mystery Gift
when you return this page...

Return this coupon and we'll send you 4 Mills & Boon® Romances from the Enchanted series and a mystery gift absolutely FREE! We'll even pay the postage and packing for you.

We're making you this offer to introduce you to the benefits of the Reader Service™– FREE home delivery of brand-new Mills & Boon Enchanted novels, at least a month before they are available in the shops, FREE gifts and a monthly Newsletter packed with information, competitions, author profiles and lots more...

Accepting these FREE books and gift places you under no obligation to buy, you may cancel at any time, even after receiving just your free shipment. Simply complete the coupon below and send it to:

MILLS & BOON READER SERVICE, FREEPOST, CROYDON, SURREY, CR9 3WZ.

READERS IN EIRE PLEASE SEND COUPON TO PO BOX 4546, DUBLIN 24

NO STAMP NEEDED

Yes, please send me 4 free Enchanted novels and a mystery gift. I understand that unless you hear from me, I will receive 6 superb new titles every month for just £2.20* each, postage and packing free. I am under no obligation to purchase any books and I may cancel or suspend my subscription at any time, but the free books and gift will be mine to keep in any case. (I am over 18 years of age)

N7YE

Ms/Mrs/Miss/Mr_____
BLOCK CAPS PLEASE

Address_____

_____

_____ Postcode _____

Jennifer
BLAKE

GARDEN
of
SCANDAL

She wants her life back...

Branded a murderer, Laurel Bancroft has
been a recluse for years. Now she wants her
life back--but someone in her past will do
anything to ensure the truth stays buried.

*"Blake's style is as steamy as a still July
night...as overwhelmingly hot as Cajun spice."*
—Chicago Tribune

MIRA®

**AVAILABLE IN PAPERBACK
FROM NOVEMBER 1997**

GET TO KNOW

THE BEST
OF ENEMIES

the latest blockbuster from TAYLOR SMITH

Who would you trust with your life? Think again.

*Linked to a terrorist bombing, a young student goes
missing. One woman believes in the girl's innocence
and is determined to find her before she is silenced.
Leya Nash has to decide—quickly—who to trust.
The wrong choice could be fatal.*

~

Valid only in the UK & Ireland against purchases made in retail outlets
and not in conjunction with any Reader Service or other offer.

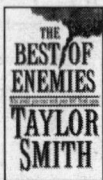

- -

THE BEST OF ENEMIES

TAYLOR SMITH

50ᵖ OFF
COUPON
VALID UNTIL: 28.2.1998

TAYLOR SMITH'S *THE BEST OF ENEMIES*

9 904170 200509

0472 00189